The Five Rules of King Zog the Terrible

(But Always Pleasant Smelling)

1. Always say "please" and "thank you."
2. Always clean up after yourself if you make a mess.
3. Never discriminate against a monster because of how it smells.
4. Never sneeze, burp, hiccup, or cough when a monster is speaking.
5. Never take anything from a monster without asking.

Unfortunately, the students were unable to follow these rules, and 10,000 monsters are now marching toward Scary School. . . .

By

DEREK THE GHOST

Scary pictures by

SCOTT M. FISCHER

HARPER

An Imprint of HarperCollinsPublishers

Library of Congress catalog card number: 2011933212
ISBN 978-0-06-196097-0 (pbk.)

Typography by Erin Fitzsimmons
13 14 15 16 17   LP/OPM   10 9 8 7 6 5 4 3 2 1
❖
First paperback edition, 2013

To Stephen King, J. K. Rowling,
Louis Sachar, Bill Watterson, Kurt
Vonnegut, and all the writers who
cracked me up, scared me witless,
and brought me to new worlds.
—Derek

Contents

Caveat discipulus

Reintroduction

W
ell, hello. It's good to see you again. In case
you forgot, my name is Derek the Ghost.

If you're reading this book, I guess that
means you liked my first book. That makes me the
happiest an eleven-year-old ghost can possibly be.

Because I like you, I'm going to let you in on a
secret. I'm standing next to you right now.

Wow. You're not even going to wave? Okay.
Whatever.

Ah, I'm just kidding. I know you can't see me. You
have to go to strange places like Scary School to be able
to see us. That makes sense to me. If people could see
ghosts, they would seriously freak out. Not good at all!

So, we're invisible when we're out and about. Don't worry though, we're cool. Well, most of us anyway.

Once *Scary School*, the first book I wrote, was finished, I thought I would get to move on, but it turned out that Scary School won a trip to meet the Monster King as the grand prize for winning the Ghoul Games. And when amazing things are happening at Scary School, it's up to me to write about them.

Actually, that just gave me an idea. After you finish reading this book, you ought to go to my website, ScarySchool.com, and write your own spooky or funny story. If I like it, I'll post it on my website for all the other kids around the world to read. Then you can call yourself a writer just like me!

Anyway, it's time for me to go back to my haunted house and prepare for another horrific year.

I wish you the best of luck in surviving this semester at Scary School. Hopefully, I'll see you after winter break, but I still can't guarantee you'll make it out alive.

Note from
Derek the Ghost

To be really in the know, go to the Secret Section of ScarySchool.com to unlock the Bonus Chapter of Book One. We're about to pick up where that chapter left off! You don't need it, but why miss it?

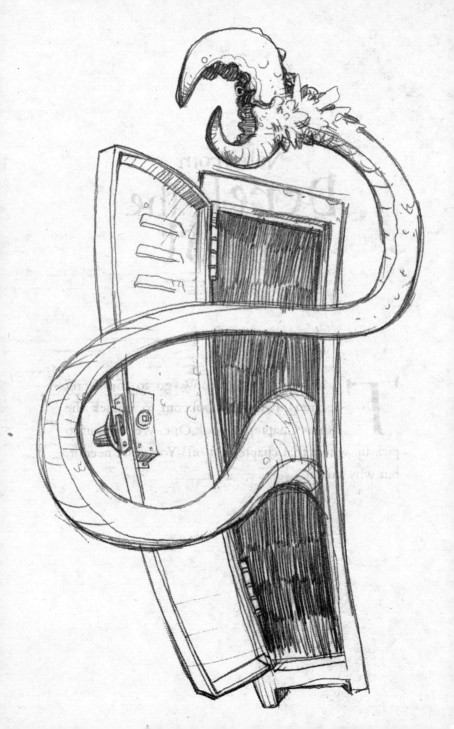

1

The Elephant Who Always Forgets

Petunia ducked frantically, barely avoiding being pulled into the Locker of Infinite Oblivion by the hideous ragged claw. It recoiled into the locker angrily, slamming the door shut.

I have got to pay closer attention, Petunia reminded herself, dusting the smudges off her purple dress.

She had gotten distracted searching the walkway for her friends.

Even though none of her classmates had contacted

her over the summer, she had been desperately looking forward to school starting so she could see them. Petunia had not even heard from her best friend, Frank (pronounced "Rachel"), which she thought was very odd.

After the first few weeks of summer, Petunia had grown so lonely that she grew her purple hair back down to her purple shoulders. Her purple hair attracted honeybees, and she needed the company.

Petunia couldn't wait to find out who her new sixth-grade teacher would be. The teachers were always special. Last year, Petunia's teacher was Ms. Fangs, an 850-year-old vampire who was very, very nice. She only bit two kids the whole year.

As Petunia walked down the twisting main hallway of Scary School, most kids backed away from the bees circling her head.

Still not seeing her classmates, Petunia was very puzzled. Eventually she saw a boy she recognized. His name was Charles Nukid. He was from the other sixth-grade class. As always, his hair was molded into a perfect hair helmet on top of his egg-shaped head. He was wearing gray shorts, a white dress shirt, and a polka-dot tie, which was the official Scary School uniform that everybody else refused to wear because it looked so stupid.

"Hi, Charles," said Petunia. "Have you seen anyone from my class?"

"No, I was actually looking for Penny. Let me know if you find her. I have to hurry or else I'll only be on time for class instead of early. I'm always early. That's my own personal rule. Why risk it, you know?"

Charles had to catch his breath. It was as if he hadn't spoken to anyone all summer and had become overexcited when the chance came.

Petunia said good-bye to Charles and skipped toward her classroom. When she stepped into the room, she dropped her books in shock.

The room was empty.

Petunia double-checked her schedule. She was in the right place, Dungeon 5B, but there were no classmates and no teacher.

At 8:00 a.m., she peeked out into the hallway. It was as empty as her classroom.

Kids are *never* late for class at Scary School, because if a teacher is in a bad mood, well, let's just say there are a few lollygaggers who are walking around without all their toes or noses.

Petunia decided to take a seat and hoped that someone would come. She didn't dare wander the hallways without a hall pass. Even though the hallway monitor, Mr. Spider-Eyes, had been eaten by Mrs. T, the

T. rex, during the Ghoul Games, the new hallway monitor might be even meaner. There was no point in taking the chance.

After a couple minutes, Petunia heard a loud thumping from the hallway.

Gathump. Gathump. Gathump. It got closer and closer, then stopped at the doorway. Petunia gulped.

Suddenly, the door burst open. In stomped something Petunia had never seen before. The creature had big, stumpy elephant feet, but the body of a man. He was wearing a tight-fitting suit and tie. His knitted

brown jacket hung loosely around his humanlike arms. The creature had the head of a giant elephant, with floppy ears, long ivory tusks, and a trunk that hung halfway down his body.

He looked at Petunia, then at a sheet of paper he was holding in his trunk.

"Hello," said the creature in a deep, goofy-sounding voice. "Are you the teacher?"

"No," Petunia answered, growing more confused by the second.

"Oh," said the creature. "Well, by process of elimination, I guess that means I'm the teacher."

Petunia stared at him blankly.

"What's your name?" the creature asked.

"Petunia."

"Petunia, eh? I'm going to write that down."

The creature placed the paper on the desk, then used his trunk to write Petunia's name on the sheet of paper. He didn't have much success as there was nothing holding the paper in place. It just kept sliding all over the desk.

The creature got frustrated. "This paper won't stay put for me to write down your name. Please excuse me if I forget it."

"Why don't you use your hands instead of your trunk?" Petunia suggested.

"Hands?" said the creature quizzically. He lifted his hands in front of his eyes and jumped back in fright. His hands were covered with fish scales.

"Oh my goodness! I have scaly hands! What kind of strange creature am I?"

"I have no idea," said Petunia.

"Well, thank you for pointing these out to me, young lady. I couldn't see them because my trunk was in the way. Tell me, what's your name?"

"Petunia."

"Petunia, eh? I'm going to write that down so I don't forget."

This time the creature used his hands to write down Petunia's name on the sheet of paper.

"Excellent!" he exclaimed. "Now we're getting somewhere. It says on this sheet of paper that my name is Morris Grump. Apparently, I'm the teacher for the sixth-grade class at Scary School. Hmm. I suppose that means you better call me Mr. Grump."

"Mr. Grump," asked Petunia, "do you know where the rest of the class is?"

"The rest of the class? No. Do you?"

"No."

"Oh. Well, we better wait here for them. I'd hate to go wandering around and get lost. I don't even think I'm supposed to be living on this continent. Don't elephants come from Africa?"

"Africa or southern Asia," Petunia replied.

"Say, you're smart! You're going to be useful!" exclaimed Mr. Grump.

"Is that what you are? An elephant?" asked Petunia. "You don't seem to be a full elephant."

"Good point," said Mr. Grump. "I seem to be part scaly man also. I guess that means I'm the Elephant Man."

"But I thought elephants never forget."

"If you say so. The last thing I remember was trudging up a snowy mountain dragging a sack of coconuts behind me. The next thing I knew, I was walking down that hallway holding this sheet of paper."

"To be honest, you don't seem to know very much for a teacher."

"Well, I'm sure I must have done something *very* impressive to earn this position. I'll certainly give it my best. Now, what's the first thing you would like me to teach you?"

"Um. I don't know. Math?"

"Excellent choice! Math it is!" Then Mr. Grump's expression went blank and his trunk went limp. "What's math?" he asked.

Ugh, Petunia thought to herself. This is going to be a long year.

7

2
The Daring Rescue

For the next hour, Petunia sat down with Mr. Grump and taught him the basics of math.

Mr. Grump wrote everything down as fast as he could, holding the paper with his hands and scribbling with his agile trunk.

When first period ended, Mr. Grump was so happy he couldn't wait for the next subject.

"What's next? What's next?" he asked excitedly, jumping up and down, causing the whole room to shake.

Petunia looked around the empty room. She was becoming very worried. There's no way the whole class would be gone the first day of school. Something must be wrong.

"We have to go find the rest of the class now," Petunia said to Mr. Grump.

"Okay," said Mr. Grump. "You lead the way."

"But I don't know where to look," said Petunia. "They could be anywhere."

"Hmmm," murmured Mr. Grump, scratching the top of his head with his trunk. "When I misplace something, which I do constantly, I always retrace my steps. Where's the last place you saw them?"

"The last place I saw them was at Jacqueline's haunted house on the last day of school. They all went into the Room of Fun, but I decided not to go in."

"Well then, that's the first place we'll look! Excellent remembering, um . . . um . . . ." Mr. Grump slyly looked at his sheet of paper. "Petunia. I won't forget it again. Let's go, ummm . . ."

"Petunia," said Petunia, rolling her eyes.

Petunia led the way to the school yard. Jacqueline's haunted house stood beside the path that leads through the playground, which some kids like to call the slayground because of the high probability of injury or demise. Take, for instance, the alligators at the bottom of the slide. Brave kids still like to ride it, though. It's a fun slide until that last part with the chomping and dismemberment.

In case you don't remember, Jacqueline is my eight-year-old sister. She'll be nine in a month. She built the haunted house for me last year so that I would have a place to haunt. The school building was so uncomfortable. I don't know how living kids can stand sitting at those desks for so long.

Petunia and Mr. Grump stepped up to the front door of the haunted house and knocked. Neither realized that I had been watching them all morning and writing everything down. Naturally, I followed them to my haunted house, whereupon I made myself visible.

Petunia knew me and said hello. Mr. Grump had apparently never seen a ghost before and got very scared.

"Gh-gh-ghooosst!" he howled. He trumpeted a deafening noise through his trunk and started stampeding across the school yard.

In his panic, he ran into a tetherball pole with a *clang*, staggered about dizzily for a few seconds, then collapsed unconscious on the lawn.

"Don't worry. Your teacher should be fine," I said to Petunia. "Please come in."

I opened the door for her and we walked into the foyer. Ghosts circled the black chandelier above the great white fountain. Petunia remembered what to do. She plucked one purple hair from her head and placed it carefully in the fountain's pool. Jets of water shot up and the ghosts cheered with joy. One flew down and opened the door to the rest of the house.

"Thank you," said Petunia.

"No, thank *you*," said the ghost, placing Petunia's hair on its white ghostly head.

As we walked down the haunted corridors, I told Petunia how lonesome I had been all summer with none of the kids around to write about. She said that she had had a very similar summer, with nothing to do but read.

"That's funny," I replied. "I couldn't read a book even if I wanted to. My hands go straight through them."

"How sad," Petunia said, trying to pat my shoulder, but whooshing right through me.

"Luckily, I have a ghost pad and a ghost pen that never runs out of ink, so I can write all I want."

We came to the end of the hallway to the door marked ROOM OF FUN.

"Is my class still in there?" Petunia asked me.

"I remember that everyone except you went in there on the last day of school. They started going down a slide and they haven't come out since."

Petunia opened the door to the Room of Fun, and a wave of sound crashed upon our ears. It sounded like a symphony of screaming and *whee*ing. Petunia bravely stepped into the pitch-black room and had to quickly catch her balance. She was standing on a ledge overlooking a deep, dark pit.

"Hello!" she called down into the pit. "Is anybody down there?"

"Petunia? Is that you?" It was the voice of her best friend, Frank, which is pronounced "Rachel."

"Yes, it's me!"

"Help us, Petunia! We've been going down this slide for three months and can't get off!"

Petunia thought it was very strange that they had been sliding downward for so long, but they were still able to hear her. At a normal rate of descent, they should have already gone straight into the Earth's core and been liquefied.

As Petunia's eyes became adjusted to the darkness, she began walking gingerly along the edge of the pit, feeling the stone wall with her hands. When she got to the other end of the room, she felt something strange. One of the blocks of stone was much warmer than the others. She knocked on the stone and it crumbled away like sand, revealing a glowing lever behind it.

As soon as Petunia pulled on the lever, the symphony of sound came to a halt. Petunia realized that the screams and *whee*s were not coming from her classmates. They were being blasted through speakers in order to mask another sound—the din of churning gears.

Lights came on, and Petunia could see into the pit. It didn't look that deep at all. Perhaps twenty feet to the bottom. Her classmates were piled on top of one another.

The walls inside the pit showed projections of a moving background so it looked and felt like they were sliding down, when in fact they were staying right in place the entire time! Just like a super-slippery treadmill.

Petunia began to recognize her classmates. There was Jason, still wearing his hockey mask. Fred, the boy without fear. The three Rachels, Wendy Crumkin, Penny Possum, Fritz, and even Ms. Fangs. They looked haggard and hungry, but were in a surprisingly good mood. Petunia guessed it was because they had been having nonstop fun for the last three months.

There were also empty water bottles and food wrappers all over the ground. Those items must have been regularly placed on the slide to keep the kids alive. My sister thought of everything.

As it dawned on the class what was really going on, most of them slapped their heads in frustration for not figuring it out sooner. Not even the teacher, Ms. Fangs, had had any clue.

The problem at the moment was that her class was still stuck at the bottom of the pit with no way to get out. Thinking quickly, Petunia sent her bees swarming down. The kids screamed, thinking they were being attacked, when in fact the bees were grabbing hold of them and airlifting them out of the pit one by one.

Soon the whole class was out of the pit. They were so grateful to Petunia that nobody made fun of her purple complexion for a whole week. Frank hugged her best friend so hard she could barely breathe.

Ms. Fangs was looking even more pale than usual.

She snatched a rat crawling along the floor and sucked out all its blood in one big gulp.

"Eeewww!" the class moaned, gawking at the disgusting display.

"Oh, it's not so bad," Ms. Fangs assured them. "Tastes like rat juice."

Wendy barfed.

As the class stepped outside into the bright sunlight, they noticed Mr. Grump lying on the ground, snoring through the side of his mouth. Petunia explained that he was their new sixth-grade teacher. The kids pulled him up off the ground. His tusks were stuck in the dirt, so it wasn't easy.

Mr. Grump opened his eyes.

"Are you okay, Mr. Grump?" Petunia asked.

"My head hurts, but I'm feeling better. Thank you, Petunia."

"Hey! You remembered my name!"

"I did, didn't I? My memory must be improving. Now if only I could remember why in the world I was dragging those coconuts up that snowy mountain!"

3
The Mummy's Curse

At the same time that Petunia was walking into an empty classroom on the first day of class, Charles Nukid was walking into a full one. There were thirty kids in the room. The only one he recognized was Cindy Chan. Together, they were the sole survivors of Dr. Dragonbreath's class last year.

When Charles entered the room, the other kids stared at him in disbelief. As always, he was the one student wearing the school uniform. Every other kid refused to wear the gray shorts, white dress shirt, and polka-dot tie as soon as they saw they looked like a clown who sold insurance. As a result, *not* wearing the school uniform became the school uniform. None of the teachers even knew what the school uniform looked like.

Charles didn't care how ridiculous he looked in this outfit. He liked obeying each rule to the letter. Ironically, many girls considered him to be a rule-breaking rebel for daring to dress the way he did, and were absolutely crazy about him. Charles didn't care about those girls, though. Penny Possum was the only one in school he considered to be his friend.

It didn't make the slightest bit of difference that Penny never spoke. They had never had a single conversation, but both had learned that there are other ways to communicate.

Penny had even managed to loosen him up a little before summer vacation by mussing up his hair. Usually, every strand had to be perfectly in place or it drove him crazy. Because he hadn't seen Penny all summer, he thought he was being punished for messing up his hair. Now he was even more finicky about keeping it neat than ever.

In this ghostwriter's humble opinion, Charles really needs to lighten up.

Several new kids were shooting spitballs across the room and chasing one another down the aisles. They had yet to learn that Scary School is no joke.

Charles took a seat next to Cindy Chan. She looked at him through her thick glasses and said, "I heard our teacher is Mr. Snakeskin. Is he mean?"

"Well," said Charles, "Mr. Snakeskin has no problem removing his own skin, so he'd probably have no problem removing our skins if we misbehave."

Charles noticed a kid with long hair over his face who was sitting all by himself in the back corner. He didn't seem to have any friends, so Charles thought he would introduce himself. But before he could, the door flew open.

Everyone froze in place.

There was a squeaking of wheels from outside the door and a large stone object was wheeled in on a dolly, pushed by a hunchback wearing black robes.

The hunchback placed the stone object in front of the class. Charles Nukid

knew what it was immediately. Standing eight feet tall, composed of thick limestone, and covered in carvings and symbols, it was a *sarcophagus*—the coffin of choice for the ancient Egyptians. It contained the mummified remains of a king who had died thousands of years ago.

The Mummy was one of Charles Nukid's favorite movies. It had led him to read many books about ancient Egypt. He could only hope all that reading would pay off now.

The hunchback pulled away the outer slab of stone, revealing the inner sarcophagus—a shining, golden encasement in the shape of a man adorned with a headdress. The statue had a long chin-beard painted black. His arms were folded across his chest. His hands were clutching a snake and a scepter.

The hunchback grumbled, "Sixth grade, Mr. Snakeskin will *not* be your teacher this year. He is only teaching gym from now on. This is your new teacher. I've been told to tell you *not* to ask how we got him. Good luck surviving your first class."

The hunchback waddled out the door, leaving the statue staring stone-faced at the class.

For several minutes nothing happened. The kids just sat in their seats waiting for the teacher to emerge from the upright coffin. But the statue just stood there, towering above them, its eyes blank and cold.

Finally, a boy with black hair named Steven Kingsley said, "Hello? Are you there, teacher?"

Then a girl sitting next to him said, "Are you alive?" Nothing.

Eventually, Bryce McCallister, the lonely-looking boy with long hair over his face, got up to investigate the golden sarcophagus. He wore baggy clothes. His hair made it impossible to tell what he looked like.

Bryce whipped the hair away from his eyes and examined the golden body.

Bryce

"Hey, there are carvings on here," he announced. "Help me clear this dust away."

A bunch of kids bounced up and started blowing the dust off the sarcophagus to reveal hidden words and hieroglyphs—the writing of the ancient Egyptians. Charles Nukid and Cindy Chan stayed in their seats, not wanting to upset their teacher—or whatever it was.

Nobody could decipher the strange symbols, but then Bryce found something written in English on a slab next to the toe. It said:

Death shall come on swift wings to he who disturbs the peace of the king.

The kids who were dusting off the sarcophagus quickly ran back to their seats. Bryce was the only kid who didn't rush back.

"You guys are a bunch of scaredy-cats," he said to the class reproachfully. "It's just an old hunk of metal. There's nothing it can do. Watch."

Bryce started hitting and slapping the sarcophagus.

"I wouldn't do that," Charles Nukid warned Bryce.

"Be quiet, Toothpick," said Bryce harshly. "I'll do what I want."

Charles hated being called Toothpick. Kids seemed

to naturally give him that name because he was so skinny.

Bryce proceeded to kick the shin of the sarcophagus. It hurt him much more than it hurt the metal. Grabbing his foot, he screeched, "Ow! Ow! Ow!"

The class laughed at him.

"Stop it!" he yelled. "At least I'm not chicken like the rest of you."

All of a sudden, there was a rumbling. Bryce saw his classmates' eyes widen and he turned his head slowly. The sarcophagus was shaking. The walls of the classroom shook with it. Several kids dived under their desks. The rest were frozen, their eyes glued to the coffin.

Then, the front of the sarcophagus began to open. A deep moaning filled the room. The dank smell of thousand-year-old death filled the air.

A decrepit hand slipped through the crack. The sound of labored breathing from inside the coffin made everyone shake with fear. With one last push, the golden sarcophagus swung open. The children gazed upon a hideous mummy. It was wrapped in tattered white bandages and reeked of decay.

"Aughghghh," the mummy moaned in despair.

The mummy reached down, rubbing his shin where Bryce had kicked him. Then, he limped out of the sarcophagus and glared at the terrified students.

"All right," said the mummy. His voice sounded like his lungs were filled with gravel and his tongue was made of sandpaper. "Who has dared to kick me in my left shin?"

None of the class pointed, but everyone looked down at Bryce, still sitting on the floor in front.

"So, it was *you*, was it?" The mummy's voice rose accusingly.

"I . . . I'm sorry," said Bryce.

"Sorry? My left shin is my bad shin! I hurt it in a game of undead soccer five hundred years ago, and it's never been the same. You've reaggravated a very, very old injury."

"I . . . I didn't know."

"Didn't know?" The mummy whipped around and pointed to the symbols on his sarcophagus. "It says right here in plain hieroglyphics that in order to wake me peacefully, all you have to do is kick my *right* shin. Don't tell me you've never learned left from right!"

"I couldn't read the symbols," Bryce answered.

"Oh no. Don't tell me none of you can read. Can *you* read?" hissed the mummy, pointing at Cindy Chan.

"I can w-w-wead Engwish when I'm wearing my

g–gwasses." Cindy always stammered when she was nervous.

"English? Feh! That's been spoken for barely a thousand years. My language dates back ten thousand years! Now *that's* a language."

The mummy flicked its hand at Bryce. "Take your seat, boy."

Bryce scurried back to his seat.

The mummy walked to the chalkboard and drew several pictures. He drew a circle, a bird, a snake, then another bird.

"This is my name, class."

A blond–haired girl sitting in the front row said, "Your name is Circle Bird Snake Bird?"

"No!" howled the mummy. "This is how you spell King Khufu in hieroglyphs. Don't any of you know who I am?"

Charles got very excited, and his hand shot up.

"Yes, you. The one out of uniform."

Charles stood up and said, "You were the pharaoh of Egypt over 4,500 years ago in the twenty-sixth century BCE. You built the Great Pyramid, which is one of the Seven Wonders of the World."

"Very good," said King Khufu. "Since you're the expert, perhaps you can tell us about the curse of the mummies?"

King
Khufu

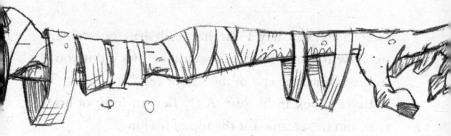

Charles gulped. What have I gotten myself into? he thought.

"Well," said Charles aloud, "Lord Carnarvon was one of the archaeologists who first opened the tomb of King Tut."

"Correct," said King Khufu. "King Tut is a good buddy of mine. What happened to that archaeologist?"

"Soon after he opened the tomb, Lord Carnarvon was bitten by a mosquito. The bite became infected and he died."

"Correct! Death always comes on swift wings to those who disturb the peace of a king. You could say that death came to Lord Carnarvon on the swift wings of a mosquito, could you not?"

Charles nodded.

Khufu continued, "Today, the slumber of a mummy has been disturbed once again . . . by *him*." Khufu pointed a rotting finger at Bryce. "A curse has been

29

placed upon you, boy. I fear that death shall soon come upon swift wings for you. I would be shocked if you survived until the end of the school year."

Bryce shook in his seat. A fly flew in front of his face, and he screamed at the top of his lungs.

"Aha!" Khufu exclaimed. "Look who's the scaredy-cat now!"

The mummy laughed, and a few brave kids laughed with him. Charles was not one of them.

For the rest of the morning, whenever someone saw a bug flying close to Bryce, they swatted it away for him. Several cute girls gave him hugs and told him to be brave. Getting cursed seemed to make him the most popular kid in school.

Up until lunch, King Khufu taught the class how to translate hieroglyphs. It wasn't nearly as difficult as the students thought it would be. They had a lot of fun learning to spell their own names in hieroglyphic. Mine is Hand-Feather-Eyeball-Feather-Cup. I'm kind of glad we use a different alphabet these days.

At the end of the day, Khufu stepped back into his sarcophagus and said, "Wake me up when it's time for class tomorrow." And he closed the stone slab over himself.

As the class was leaving, Charles Nukid stayed behind and read the hieroglyphs on the sarcophagus. He immediately burst into laughter.

"Hey, Bryce!" Charles shouted.

Bryce jumped back, startled. "What? Is there a beetle flying near me?"

"No, Bryce. It says here: 'In order to wake the pharaoh peacefully, kick him in his right *or* left shin.' I think King Khufu was just messing with you to teach you a lesson."

"Oh," said Bryce, the weight of the world dropping off his shoulders. "Tell you what, I'll owe you a big favor if you don't tell anyone. Since they heard I'm going to die, everyone's being super nice to me!"

4
The Big Announcement

By the third day of school, the new students had settled into a daily routine of learning, horror, and mayhem. Satisfied, Principal Headcrusher thought it was a good time to make the big announcement.

She gently gripped a microphone in her salad-bowl-sized hands, and her voice sounded on a PA system in every classroom.

"Attention, students and faculty. After lunch, everyone is to report to Petrified Pavilion for a big surprise."

All the veteran students groaned because they hated

surprises. At Scary School a surprise often meant that you would be turned into a mouse or lose an essential body part.

During the Italian-themed lunch, Sue the Amazing Octo-Chef's delicious spaghetti and eyeballs had Jason and Fred going back for seconds. The side of garlic toast sent several vampire kids to Nurse Hairymoles's office. I enjoyed a gourmet ghost-cheese pizza.

Once lunch was finished, the students gathered on the enormous wooden hands of Petrified Pavilion. They were raised into its screaming mouth, which was the entrance to the magnificent auditorium.

Charles sat next to Petunia, Raychel sat next to Rachael, and Bryce sat next to six girls from his class. They were shielding him from mosquitoes.

Lindsey sat next to her friends Stephanie and Maria. She still wore blond pigtails, but was now considered the nicest girl in school after being the meanest girl last year.

Once all were seated, Principal Headcrusher walked across the stage. She was wearing a very fashionable salmon-pink pantsuit. Her frizzy black hair looked like she had just been electrocuted.

She stepped up to a podium and grasped the microphone with her massive hands. The microphone exploded into dust.

"Whoops," she said. "Oh well, this will work better anyway."

Principal Headcrusher raised her hands to her mouth, which amplified her voice more than any microphone could. Experienced students stuck their fingers in their ears. New students heard ringing for the next three weeks.

"Good afternoon, vampires, zombies, werewolves, and you less fortunate human students," Principal Headcrusher announced. "Who here remembers what the grand prize was for winning the Ghoul Games last spring?"

Wendy Crumkin, a smart girl with freckles, glasses, and braided red hair, raised her hand.

"Yes, Wendy?"

Wendy stood up and answered confidently, "The grand prize was a trip to Albania to meet the Monster King."

"That is correct!" Principal Headcrusher declared.

The students erupted in cheers.

"Except for one thing."

The students became silent.

"It's not a trip to Albania. But you're close. It's a trip to Albany."

"But last year you said Albania."

"I did? Well, I meant Albany."

The students looked at one another in confusion.

"Where's Albany?" Bryce McCallister asked aloud.

"Good question. It's a town in upstate New York."

"So we're going to New York!" Lindsey exclaimed with excitement. "I've always wanted to see Broadway!"

"No, no, no," said Principal Headcrusher. "Albany is very far from New York City. But don't worry, it is very similar to New York City, just without all the attractions and fun things to do. You'll love it."

The students groaned.

Later that day, each teacher handed out permission slips. The students had to have their parents sign off on their "fantastic" trip to Albany. The plan was to leave a week from Monday and return that Friday. The parents were only too happy to sign off on the trip to a harmless place like Albany and almost all of them were secretly thrilled to have a whole week to themselves.

Just kidding. Not *almost* all the parents. Absolutely *all* the parents were thrilled.

On Thursday morning, the new hall monitor, Ms. Hydra, wheeled all the signed permission slips into Principal Headcrusher's office in a big red wagon.

Principal Headcrusher was very proud of the new Scary School hall monitor. Who better to be a hall monitor than Ms. Hydra—a giant monitor lizard with nine fearsome heads? Each head was attached to a twenty-foot scaly neck that could twist and bend around corners. The nine necks were attached to a stout lizard body.

"Thank you, Ms. Hydra," said Principal Head-crusher, taking the permission slips. "Anything to report?"

The fifth of Ms. Hydra's nine heads slithered forward and said with a serpentine hiss, "Thisss morning I ssssaw a boy out of uniform. He was wearing gray shorts, a white dress shirt, and a polka-dot tie! Nobody ever wears *that*! The nerve of him!"

"It must have been Charles Nukid. You didn't eat him, did you?"

"No, I had three helpings of maggot pancakes for breakfast. Lucky for him I was full. So I sent him to Ms. T for detention."

"Okay, that's fine. But for future reference, Charles is actually the only student who wears the school uniform. All the other children refuse to wear it because it looks so atrocious. I did that on purpose, you see."

"On purposse? Why?"

"I am secretly keeping track of all the students who don't wear the school uniform. If any parents complain that their child was turned into a zombie or fell

37

into the lava pool or got
their fingers bitten
off by the Venus
flytraps, I can
say, 'Look. Your
child has been out of uniform three
hundred days in a row. What did
you expect?' And that settles the issue."

Ms. Hydra's seventh head said, "That's a ssssssuper
idea. I guess that's why you're the principal."

"Oh, stop being such a sssssssuck-up!" said the
third head.

"I'm thirsty!" said the second head.

"You're always thirsty," said the eighth head. "Why
don't you remember to bring a water bottle?"

"Hey, we share the same pockets. You forgot the water too!" replied the second head.

Principal Headcrusher finally butted in.
"That will be all, Ms. Hydra. Please go back
to patrolling the hallways."

"Yesss, right away," piped the seventh head.

"No, wait!" said the fifth head. "There's that other
thing."

"Oh, right," said the first head. "Principal, we
heard that you were taking the sssstudents to meet the
Monster King."

Ms. Hydra

"That's right," said Principal Headcrusher.

"Do you think that's a good idea? Haven't you heard the sssstory?"

Principal Headcrusher leaned forward with keen interest.

"What story?" she asked.

Ms. Hydra's nine heads started swiveling back and forth to make sure nobody was eavesdropping. A bead of sweat dripped down each of her nine necks.

"What story?" Principal Headcrusher prodded.

5

King Zog the Terrible (But Always Pleasant Smelling)

"The story of King Zog the Terrible," all of Ms. Hydra's nine heads whispered as one.

The second head added, "But Always Pleasant Smelling."

The other eight heads nodded in agreement about King Zog's ever-present pleasant odor.

At that point, all nine of Ms. Hydra's heads began

telling the story of King Zog's rise to power. When she finished, Principal Headcrusher ordered Ms. Hydra to tell the story to every class. The details would undoubtedly save many students' lives.

Ms. Hydra entered Mr. Grump's sixth-grade class. Having a twenty-foot monitor lizard with nine heads enter the class unannounced was so horrifying, the class ducked under their desks and covered their heads. Mr. Grump had no idea who Ms. Hydra was (even though they had had a pleasant conversation that morning). He trumpeted his snout in fear and jumped out the window. Fred, the boy the without fear, was the only one who remained seated at his desk, still totally certain he was dreaming.

The class was too afraid of Ms. Hydra to pay close attention to her story, so I decided to take over. Ms. Hydra went to King Khufu's class, who were more used to learning from a terrifying teacher.

"To begin with," I said to Mr. Grump's class, "you'll need to know what defines a monster. There are many well-known species of monsters, but there is one common trait that unites them: They all smell terrible."

The class laughed, thinking about stinky monsters.

I continued, "Each monster has a unique odor. It can smell like a combination of skunk juice, spoiled cheese, sweaty feet, rotting fish, boiled liver, or dinosaur burps. The smellier the creature, the more respected it is in the monster community.

"In the history of monsters, only the ones with the foulest odor have ever become a king or queen. That's why when Zog was born smelling like fresh-baked cookies, rushing waterfalls, and fields of lavender in springtime, nobody gave him much of a chance to amount to anything."

The girls cooed, thinking about those lovely smells.

"Zog was born with the head of a giant toad, the body of a walrus, and the tail of a scorpion. By the looks of him, he should have smelled atrocious, but the more he rolled in muck and filth, the more he smelled like a summer breeze in a peach orchard.

"His parents hoped that his foul odor would develop with age, but it didn't. After several years, he still smelled like a barrel of sweet potpourri. One day, the Monster Patrol sniffed out his appallingly pleasant odor and locked him away in the Dungeon of Rot until he started smelling like a real monster.

"Heartbroken, Zog's parents bravely stormed the dungeon to free their son. They managed to break a hole in the wall with their mighty nose horns, giving Zog an opening to escape.

"Zog ran as fast as he could through Monster Forest,

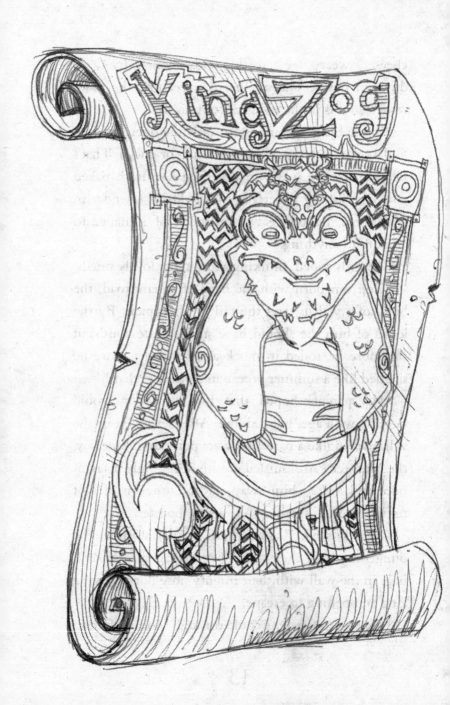

using all the strength of his horse legs. Did I mention Zog has horse legs? He has horse legs. The patrol monsters frantically chased after him, but in the end, he managed to outrun them. His parents, however, were not so fast and were captured and locked away in the dungeon."

The class was sad, thinking about what they would do if they were left without parents.

"Lost and alone, Zog wandered the wilderness until he found a hidden valley. It turned out, a whole society of sweet-smelling monsters was living there. They liked Zog and decided to adopt him."

The class exhaled in relief that Zog had found a new family.

"Scared of being discovered, the monsters kept quiet at all times. They tried to become as unmonsterlike as possible and had very good manners. They always ate their meals with a fork and knife. They said 'excuse me' when they belched, which was often.

"When Zog reached adulthood, he was elected leader of the sweet-smelling monsters. But rather than having them practice their manners, Zog began training the monsters in combat. Did I mention Zog's father was a karate master who gave Zog karate lessons every day? Zog's father was a karate master who gave Zog karate lessons every day.

"Soon, Zog was in command of an army of warriors whom he called karate monsters. They were tough, but smelled like cake batter whisking in a French bakery. One of those monsters was Ms. Stingbottom, the fluffy pink monster with the head of a lion who taught us Monster Math last year.

"Zog had never stopped missing his parents. He was bent on seeing them again to say thank you for freeing him.

"On a windy summer day, Zog's army stormed across the countryside until they reached the castle of Bub-Gub, the Monster King.

"The palace guards fought fiercely, but hopelessly. Their undisciplined gnashing of teeth and flailing of claws was no match for well-trained karate monsters.

"The army had soon made its way into the dungeon, where Zog's parents were chained to the wall. Breaking their bonds, Zog hugged his parents so hard he nearly crushed them. Together, they roared with joy. If monsters had a word for love, they would have certainly said 'I love you' a thousand times.

"Overrun, Bub-Gub the Monster King surrendered to Zog and pronounced him the new king of the monsters.

"Thus began the reign of King Zog. His first decree was that all monsters were to be treated equally, whether they smelled like a rotting troll carcass or blooming cherry trees.

"Now, you are probably wondering why Zog is called King Zog the Terrible when he seems to have done so much good. Here is why:

"Along with his first decree, Zog also made another decree. He enjoyed the customs of the peaceful valley and declared that all monsters must practice perfect manners at all times. Failure to say please or thank you would lead to immediate punishment. An offender would be dismembered or eaten, depending on the offense.

"Zog gave one seminar on perfect manners and then everyone was on their own. Many monsters lost their lives the next day when they burped at the dining table, picked food from their teeth, or forgot to write a thank-you note after receiving a gift.

"One day, the newly formed Monster Manners Patrol caught five of Ms. Hydra's heads staring at a good-looking dragon for more than three seconds. Staring was considered impolite and the Monster Patrol began chasing after her. Ms. Hydra had to flee for her life, leaving all of her friends and belongings behind.

"So, even though there was a new king, things were still really bad. Only in a different way."

After I finished telling the story to Mr. Grump's class, Petunia said, "We certainly can't refuse the Monster King's invitation to visit him. He would be insulted and could attack us."

Jason added, "But if any of us makes a mistake in our manners, we could be . . ."

"Dismembered or eaten. Depending on the offense," I answered.

"Well, I guess that's better than having the whole school attacked by an army of karate monsters," said the smartest girl in class, Wendy Crumkin. "When we visit the king, we'll just have to behave well enough to *not* get dismembered."

The rowdiest boys in class—Johnny, Ramon, and Peter—looked at their bodies and thought, Well, limbs, it was nice knowing you.

6

Tanya
Tarantula

On the fourth day of school, nobody had ever heard of Tanya Tarantula. By the fifth day of school, not only did everyone know her, she was the most popular girl at school. Despite the fact that she was a giant tarantula.

When you think of a giant tarantula, you probably think of one the size of a baseball. Or, if you're really imaginative, perhaps the size of a basketball. In either case, you're not even close.

On the fifth day of school, King Khufu asked the class, "Who can name the longest ruling female pharaoh of ancient Egypt?"

At that moment, a tarantula the size of a shopping cart fell through the ceiling right on top of Bryce McCallister.

Everyone in class screamed, thinking death upon swift wings was about to come to Bryce. But Tanya was more afraid of the students than they were of her. She jumped onto the floor and scurried all over the room, trying to find a place to hide.

The students stood on their desks in fright, causing Tanya to display her fangs and raise her legs in defense.

Charles Nukid was so scared, all of his hairs stood

Tanya

up on end. He had to spend the rest of the day putting them back into place.

The children continued screaming until King Khufu ordered, "*Silence!*" Everyone immediately hushed up. Khufu pulled out a golden sword from his sarcophagus and slowly approached the quivering Tanya.

Khufu was about to strike, so Tanya said the only thing she could think to say. She said, "Hatshepsut."

"What did you say?" asked Khufu.

"Hatshepsut."

"God bless you," said Cindy Chan.

"No," King Khufu interjected, "Hatshepsut is the answer to my question—the longest ruling female pharaoh of ancient Egypt. How remarkable."

King Khufu continued to pepper Tanya with questions, and she got every one of them right.

Maybe you're wondering how a giant tarantula could possibly know those answers. We will have to delve deeper into the life of this very special arachnid to discover the answers.

To begin with, it is important to note that Tanya Tarantula never met her parents. The reason she never met her parents was because they were also giant tarantulas. Giant tarantulas are notoriously awful parents. In fact, as soon as their tarantula children are born, they consider their parenting job done and they abandon them to survive on their own.

If your parents aren't giant tarantulas, you should consider yourself *very* lucky.

Until the moment Tanya was born, she had amazing parents. Her mom had laid a batch of five hundred eggs inside a very tight crevice on the side of a mountain on the outskirts of Monster Forest. Within the crevice, the eggs were protected from the elements. The only thing they were not safe from were the hundreds of monsters who could smell the eggs and would do anything to eat them.

For three long months, Tanya's parents, who were each about the size of the average camping tent, bravely fought off every monster who came to eat their eggs. The egg sacs were clear, so Tanya and her 499 brothers and sisters watched with pride as their parents took down monsters twice their size.

Tanya and her siblings were sure that once they hatched, they would have the best parents in the world.

On a summer morning the baby tarantulas emerged from their egg sacs. Their parents were overjoyed seeing every last one hatch unharmed. None had been eaten by a serpentiger or a jabberfox.

Each baby giant tarantula was about the size of a starfish, which is about the size of a normal full-grown tarantula. They crawled out from the crevice and smelled the fresh air and felt the soft wind. The sensitive tarantula hairs that covered their brown-and-black bodies were like millions of specialized eyes, ears, and noses, telling them every detail about their surroundings.

Sadly, the one thing they did not sense was their parents. As is the natural instinct of all tarantulas, the parents abandoned their children as soon as they were born. I can't say I blame them. If I suddenly had five hundred children crying for attention, I'd probably run for the hills too. Hey, don't judge. I'm only eleven!

When they
couldn't find their
parents, confusion quickly
turned to fear. No longer did they
have their mighty protectors.

Unfortunately, their presence on the rock face was
sensed by a different kind of creature—the tarantula
hawk. You probably think that a tarantula hawk is a
very nasty kind of bird that feeds on tarantulas. Well,

that's only half right. The tarantula hawk is actually a two-inch wasp that stings a tarantula into paralysis, then lays its eggs inside the stiff tarantula carcass for its larvae to grow inside and feast upon. The fact that it's called a tarantula hawk instead of a tarantula wasp is another example of our ridiculous language often-times causing needless confusion.

The swarm of tarantula hawks descended upon the five hundred baby giant tarantulas. Tanya's brothers and sisters laughed because they were three times the size of the tarantula hawks and were sure those bugs stood no chance against them.

Tanya, however, was quite a bit smarter than her brothers and sisters. She realized that if such small crea-tures were so willing to attack them, then they *must* have a secret weapon. She pleaded for her brothers and sisters to take cover on the ground underneath a fallen branch. Only nine of her brothers and sisters joined her.

The rest remained to battle the tarantula hawks. It did not go well. The tarantulas raised their front legs and displayed their fangs (also known as chelicerae), but the tarantula hawks flew down with dizzying speed and delivered swift stings on the tarantulas' vulnerable abdomens. All of Tanya's siblings that had chosen to stay were stung, paralyzed, and dragged off by the merciless tarantula hawks to become incubators and first meals for the tarantula hawk larvae.

Now, in the last book I mentioned that Scary School is without a doubt the most wholesome book series to be published in the last twenty years because of the important life lessons learned in the act of losing one's life. This remains true: The baby tarantulas learned several important life lessons that day.

They learned that when you're a wild animal, following your instincts instead of your emotions is usually the best move. They also learned never to judge another creature by its size. Sometimes the smallest can be the most dangerous.

Tragically, those tarantulas would never get to apply those life lessons because they were all dead, but the lessons were learned nonetheless.

Tanya and her nine remaining siblings made their way across the leafy ground into the dark wilderness of Monster Forest. They crawled across the forest floor until they reached a rotting tree stump. There, they enjoyed their first meal of creamy, sour termites.

Tanya looked at each of her siblings, and suddenly, an instinct kicked in to lead a life of complete solitude. As her siblings looked at her, she knew they were feeling the same thing.

The baby giant tarantulas nodded in acknowledgment that it had been fun enjoying one meal together as a family. In the next instant, each turned around and scampered off in a different direction. They would never see one another again.

For many weeks Tanya survived by her wits in Monster Forest. During the day, she hid inside logs and leaf piles. At night she would go out hunting for tasty crickets, beetles, and caterpillars. After one month she had doubled in size and was as big as a football.

One summer day she was sleeping in a leaf pile when she felt a disturbance in the air.

She heard a monster call out, "Here I go. Watch this!"

The large monster made a running jump into the leaf pile. Tanya dashed out in the nick of time. The monster saw her.

"Oofa," said Larry the gargoyle. "I've always wanted a pet tarantula."

The gargoyle picked up Tanya and began gently petting her. Tanya wanted to bite the gargoyle, but she worried that her venom might not affect such a large creature. It would probably just get mad and squash her.

The monsters were gargoyles on summer vacation from guarding Petrified Pavilion at Scary School.

Harry the gargoyle looked at Tanya, remarking,

"Oooh, it *is* cute. Let's keep it."

They put Tanya in a basket and gave her the name Tanya. Tanya was not happy about being kept as the gargoyles' pet, but she remembered what had happened to 490 of her brothers and sisters. Things could be worse.

When the school year began, the gargoyles returned to Scary School. They kept Tanya with them atop Petrified Pavilion so that they always had something to play with. The gargoyles were nice enough, but Tanya still wanted to be alone.

By winter, Tanya had doubled in size and was as big as a large dog. Fortune struck when the gargoyles saw a group of kids trying to sneak into Petrified Pavilion and took off after them. Tanya used the opportunity to make her escape.

She carefully crawled down the enormous, screaming face of Petrified Pavilion to the grassy area below. She scuttled as fast as she could toward the only place that looked inviting—the Scary School main building.

She made her way through a bulkhead and found herself in the Scary School basement. The damp darkness made her feel right at home.

Tanya explored her surroundings, finding a ventilation shaft in the wall. She crawled into the shaft and discovered that it snaked through every room in the school. Her favorite pastime became traveling from class to class and listening in on the lessons. She found that she loved learning. She taught herself how to write with her fangs and even took the tests right along with the students.

After a few years, Tanya was a proud straight-A student. She would have been valedictorian of Scary School had anybody known that she existed.

Most impressively, Tanya had taught herself to speak English. At night in the basement, she would practice speaking when not feasting on mice and rats. Her voice was very raspy and unladylike. Sometimes the school janitor, Marvin, would hear her, but he just assumed it was a ghost and thought nothing of it.

By the fifth day of school this year, Tanya had grown so big and heavy, she broke through the ceiling vent and came crashing down on top of Bryce McCallister.

After the incident, she found herself in front of Principal Headcrusher being grilled with more questions. After Tanya told her story, Principal Headcrusher asked, "Tanya, how would you like to be a full-time student here at Scary School? I suppose you can attend for free since you've saved me a fortune in vermin-exterminator fees over the years. As long as you keep up the good work in that department, I see no reason why you can't enroll as a student and we'll call it even."

Tanya wiggled her chelicerae (also known as fangs) up and down, which in tarantula-speak is equivalent to nodding.

That afternoon, Tanya became an official member of King Khufu's class. Since she couldn't fit into any of the chairs, they set up a lovely terrarium for her at the back of the room. When she knew an answer, she would raise one of her hairy tarantula arms. When she *really* wanted to answer a question, she raised six of her hairy arms.

After a few classes, the students stopped looking behind them every few minutes to check if she was about to pounce. She became just another member of the class.

After her first week, she found that her usual instinct of solitude was fading away. To her surprise, she was enjoying being part of a community. All the kids in class became friends with her and had a lot of fun patting her on her hairy head and riding on her back during recess. If this was what having a family felt like, she wanted more of it.

When she'd go back down to her basement at night, she'd think about all her friends who were spending time with their mothers and fathers. She wondered if her parents were out there some-where and if they still loved her.

When Tanya was invited to join her classmates on the trip to Monster Forest to meet the Monster King, she was very excited. She wasn't very homesick, but just maybe she'd see her parents there and they would give her a big, hairy eight-armed hug.

7

The Legend of Steven Kingsley

The morning when the students of Scary School were to take their trip to meet the Monster King, Steven Kingsley was shaking in his boots.

A member of King Khufu's class with Charles Nukid, he had thick black hair that draped across his forehead. His eyes were as blue as the feathers of a jagalark. Trust me. That's *really* blue.

It was raining outside and Steven was wearing a big rubbery raincoat, galoshes, rain boots, and a rain hat. The students were rushing past him in a frenzy of excitement to get on the bus that would take them to see the Monster King, but Steven couldn't move an inch. He was scared to death of going to meet the Monster King. A crash of thunder rumbled in the sky, and Steven jumped backward in fright.

Poor Steven was afraid of everything. *Everything.* He had every phobia there ever was and he even had some new phobias they had to give names to because of him.

He was afraid of the dark and afraid of the light. He was afraid of heights and afraid of being on the ground. He was afraid of ants and afraid of anteaters. He was afraid of dust and afraid of dusters. They named that fear "dusterbustaphobia."

You'd probably think Scary School was the worst possible school for Steven to attend, but the fact is, Steven was afraid of everything at his normal school anyway, so it didn't make much difference. At his previous school he was afraid of the marker boards and the erasers. He was afraid of the teachers and the janitors. He was afraid of the lockers and the lunches and the library, and none of those things had ever tried to eat a kid, as they often do at Scary School.

Steven's parents figured, Well, since he's afraid of everything anyway, why not put him in the scariest

Steven
Kingsley

school possible? Then, perhaps, everything else won't seem so scary.

Everyone thought this was a great idea. Everyone, of course, except for Steven, who was almost as angry as he was terrified at the idea of attending Scary School.

He was in Ms. Fangs's class last year, but asked to be transferred to the other class this year because too many of his classmates were Scary kids. While his new classmates weren't as scary, King Khufu was as terrifying as thirty Peter the Wolfs, so Steven wasn't much calmer.

Steven made it through the days by focusing on the two things he loved most: writing and baseball. Whenever Steven became overwhelmed with fear, he found a quiet corner where he would either write a story or watch baseball highlights on his phone.

Sometimes students would ask him what he was writing, but he was too afraid of the other kids to answer. Instead, he left copies of his stories around the school without writing his name on them. Steven didn't want anyone to know he was the author because he was afraid his peers would hate what he wrote about. Regardless, every student knew they were Steven's stories and they really liked them.

Nobody ever complimented Steven for fear he would stop writing the stories if his secret was out.

But as I was saying, on the morning when Scary School was to leave on the journey to visit the Monster King, a crash of thunder made Steven jump backward against the lockers. Unfortunately for Steven, the locker he jumped backward against was Locker 39, the most dangerous locker of all. It is also known as the Locker of Infinite Oblivion.

A wretched green claw reached out from the locker as soon as it felt Steven's presence. It wrapped itself around Steven's body and began pulling him inside.

Steven screamed as loud as he could, which attracted the attention of Ms. Hydra, the hall monitor. Ms. Hydra rushed toward Steven as fast she could, each of her nine heads determined to save him.

The other students cleared the area. Steven was holding on to the locker's edge with all his strength. The slightest slip, and he would be lost into the Oblivion.

But Ms. Hydra arrived in the nick of time and wrapped one of her twenty-foot necks around Steven. She tugged and pulled but didn't have much leverage with her stumpy legs. Steven was moments from being yanked away.

Then, to everyone's surprise, Dr. Dragonbreath

arrived on the scene. He was the meanest teacher at Scary School, having eaten twenty-six students so far this year. Compared with last year, he seemed to be losing his appetite.

Dr. Dragonbreath grabbed Ms. Hydra's legs with his strong dragon arms and pulled with all his might.

Steven didn't know what he was more afraid of—the monster grabbing on to him or the monsters trying to save him.

Even with Dr. Dragonbreath's help, Steven was slipping away. Some of the students in the hallway rushed to lend a hand. Fred, the boy without fear, clutched Dr. Dragonbreath's legs. Jason, still sporting his ever-present hockey mask, grabbed on to Fred. Charles Nukid grabbed on to Jason, Penny Possum grabbed on to Charles, Petunia grabbed on to Penny, Frank (which is pronounced "Rachel") grabbed on to Petunia, Johnny grabbed on to Frank, Peter grabbed on to Johnny, Ramon grabbed on to Peter, and Rachael grabbed on to Ramon. As soon as Rachael had grabbed on to Ramon, his zombie body broke apart into thirty pieces, and Rachael and Raychel had to help put him back together.

The tug-of-war was on for the life of poor Steven Kingsley. Nobody wanted to lose the school's favorite writer to the Infinite Oblivion. If I could physically grab on to something, I would have been pulling also, even though he's my competition.

With all the students, Dr. Dragonbreath, and Ms. Hydra pulling backward, they made some progress. Steven was coming back into view. Whatever was attached to the arm inside the locker roared angrily.

That's when another wretched claw appeared. It was holding a can of spray grease!

Laughing, the claw sprayed grease all over the area where Ms. Hydra was coiled around Steven. The area became super-lubricated and Steven slipped through Ms. Hydra's neck hold like a wet fish.

The sudden break in tension caused the students, Dr. Dragonbreath, and Ms. Hydra to fall backward on top of one another.

The claw laughed victoriously and slammed the locker door, and poor Steven was lost in the Oblivion, whence no kid has ever escaped.

Until now. . . .

8

Inside Locker 39

As soon as the locker slammed shut, many of the students started crying because they would never get to read Steven Kingsley's stories again. Petunia was especially broken up. Steven's stories made her feel better when the other students would tease her for being purple and swarming with bugs. She wanted to tell Steven how much his words meant to her, but she had been too scared. Now she would never get the chance.

Everyone, even Principal Headcrusher, tried to open the locker, but they couldn't.

Nobody felt much in the mood to go visit the Monster King anymore.

Then, Locker 39 began shaking. Sounds of gurgling and bubbling echoed through the locker's thin vents. Miraculously, the locker swung open with a loud *bluuuuuuurp!*

A slush of slime spilled out into the hallway. Steven Kingsley rode the slime like a wave crashing on the shore. Steven sucked in air as everyone looked at him in shock and relief. Then he said the last thing anybody expected him to say:

"What . . . what day is it?" Steven asked, wiping the yucky slime from his face.

Everyone looked at him, bewildered. Petunia answered, "It's September fifth."

"Is that the day we were supposed to visit the Monster King?"

"Yes. What day do you think it is?"

"I have no idea. But I was definitely inside that locker for over a year."

"*Over a year?*" several kids exclaimed. "Are you crazy?"

"No!" Steven snapped back. "The depths of the locker must be a realm outside of our space-time continuum. What felt like a year to me passed instantaneously in this world."

"Wow! Where were you?" Charles Nukid prodded, fueled by the excitement that he was in the middle of a real-life science fiction story.

"I was in the worst place imaginable," said Steven, standing up and walking slowly toward the group. He even helped up Dr. Dragonbreath and Ms. Hydra, showing no fear whatsoever. "To put it simply, I was placed smack-dab in the middle of my deepest fears and my darkest nightmares."

The kids' jaws dropped and they gathered in a circle around Steven. Even Dr. Dragonbreath and Ms. Hydra listened intently.

"I found myself in a grand hotel. It was three times as big as this school. It was deserted and outside there was a great snowstorm. I was all alone, until a man appeared carrying an ax. At first I was glad to see someone else, but then the man started chasing me! He was trying to chop me into pieces!"

The students gasped, and Ms. Hydra squeezed Dr. Dragonbreath's arm tightly. Dr. Dragonbreath turned and made eye contact with Ms. Hydra's ninth head. The ninth head winked, and Dr. Dragonbreath flashed his toothy dragon grin. Ms. Hydra's other eight heads became jealous and snipped to each other, "She was always the good-looking one."

Steven continued, "Finally, after weeks of being chased, I locked the ax-wielding madman outside the hotel and he froze in the snow."

The students let out a sigh of relief.

"But then came the worst part."

Everyone braced themselves.

"I found myself in an abandoned city. The streetlights flickered on and off, and all the stores were deserted. A tennis ball sat on the street. For days all I did was throw the tennis ball against the walls of the buildings. Then, the ball got away from me and rolled into a gutter. I went to go fish it out, but inside the gutter was a smiling clown!"

Dr. Dragonbreath and three of Ms. Hydra's heads fainted.

"It looked like Ronald McDonald, except when it smiled, I saw it had fangs. Either Ronald had a really bad dentist or this clown was *evil*. I wouldn't have eaten its french fries if they were the last food on Earth. It gestured for me to crawl into the gutter with it to get my ball. I screamed, 'No way!' and started running. When I looked behind me, I saw the clown crawling out of the gutter. Then it turned into a giant spider and started chasing after me! That's when I noticed a car with keys in the ignition. Luckily, I always paid close attention when my parents drove. I sped off in the car, but the spider was fast and remained on my tail. As I headed up a steep mountain, I decided to put the car in reverse. The spider was not expecting that. I hit it with the back of the car and it went tumbling down the mountain."

Everyone cheered.

"Unfortunately, driving backward was harder than I thought, and I also went tumbling down the mountain. Next thing I knew, I woke up in a small room with nothing in it but a bed and desk. There was just one window, with a fifty-foot drop to the ground. A big, scary lady walked inside and dropped a whole stack of papers on the desk. 'Do all your homework if you want your dinner!' she yelled.

"With nothing else to do, I sat at the desk and did the homework. It was the worst kind of homework. Tedious and boring. It made the minutes feel like hours. When I was finished, she brought me a piece of moldy bread and some wilted spinach. The scary lady had rescued me from the car wreck, but only so she could lock me in a room and force me to do nothing but grueling homework the rest of my life!"

At the mention of that, every other student passed out.

Without an audience, Steven shrugged his shoulders and walked away. The only one who didn't faint was me because I'm a ghost and don't have any blood in my head.

I made myself visible and said, "Excuse me, do you mind telling me how you escaped? It's for my book."

"Oh, you're a writer too?" Steven inquired.

"Yes. A ghostwriter actually."

"Oh, cool. Here's how I escaped: Each time I finished a homework assignment, I tore off the tiniest sliver of paper from the side of the page so it wasn't even noticeable. As the months went by, I tied the slivers of paper into a sturdy rope and was able to climb out the window to the ground below. I ran to freedom alongside a creek of mucky, slimy water. I stopped when I saw something shining in the water. When I examined it closer, I realized it was the other side of Locker 39. I stomped on the locker door and fell through into the hallway along with all the muck and slime. That's how I ended up here."

"Wow," I said. "All those scary things that happened to you would make great stories. You should write them down!"

"That's the dumbest idea I've ever heard," Steven replied, furrowing his brow. "I hate being scared. Why would I want to scare other people with my writing? I may become a writer, but I'm going to write nothing but happy stories about rainbows and kittens where nothing bad *ever* happens. Now, I don't know about you, but I can't wait to meet the Monster King. Let's go."

As Steven walked away, he stepped right over Ms. Hydra and Dr. Dragonbreath without even flinching.

I guess after living in Locker 39 for all that time, nothing else was very scary to Steven.

Not even Scary School.

Journey to the Monster King

After Steven Kingsley escaped from Locker 39, everyone made their way to the front lawn of Scary School for the big send-off.

Archie the giant squid popped his enormous eyeball out of the moat that surrounded the school to witness the festivities.

Petunia, who had just been elected class president for rescuing everyone from Jacqueline's haunted house, led her class to the front of the lawn. Mr. Grump followed behind them so he wouldn't get lost. Next, Bryce McCallister led King Khufu's sixth-grade class in a line next to Petunia's class. The class had elected Bryce president because they believed he was still cursed to die at any moment and felt sorry for him.

No one was more thrilled to meet the Monster King than Charles Nukid. Charles had heard about the strict rules one must obey to survive Monster Kingdom. He couldn't wait to arrive and start following them.

When all the classes had taken their places on the lawn, Principal Headcrusher stepped forward to address the crowd. "Good morning," she said. "Who's excited to go see the Monster King?"

The whole school cheered.

"Who's excited about taking a ten-hour bus ride?"

There was a smattering of unsure applause.

"Well, you're in luck, because we aren't taking buses. Look!"

Principal Headcrusher pointed to the sky, and a whole brigade of young dragons burst through the clouds and flew down to the front lawn. The students went crazy with excitement.

"As a thank-you for being such good hosts for last year's Ghoul Games, these dragon-students from Firecrest Middle School have offered to fly everyone to Albania to meet the Monster King!"

"Don't you mean Albany?" Wendy Crumkin corrected.

"Nope. We're going to Albania. I
had to tell your parents you were going
to Albany so they would sign the permission slips.
None of them would have let you go to Albania, and
your absence would have been a dire insult to the
Monster King. Sorry to mislead you, but I probably
saved all your lives by doing so."

Most students were used to surprises like this and
shrugged off the change in plans.

"And speaking of saving your lives," Principal
Headcrusher continued, "these are King Zog's five
most important rules. I wanted to wait to tell them to
you so that they would be fresh in your heads.

"The rules are:

"Always say please and thank you.

"Always clean up after yourself if you make a mess.

"Never discriminate against a monster because of
how it smells.

"Never sneeze, burp, hiccup, or cough when a
monster is speaking.

"And lastly, never take anything from a monster without asking."

Charles Nukid made a mental note of each rule. He kind of hoped he would have to sneeze at some point just so he could hold it in and follow Rule Number Four.

Principal Headcrusher continued, "Everyone find a buddy and ride two per dragon."

A flock of girls rushed to Charles Nukid and asked to ride with him, unable to contain their giggles. Students from last year still viewed him as Scary School's bad-boy rebel for being the only kid brave enough to wear gray shorts, a white dress shirt, and a polka-dot tie.

Charles moved through the sea of girls to find his one true friend—the only one he wanted to ride with. He didn't care for all the attention and knew that the girls only liked him because they thought he was breaking the rules, when in truth he was the only one following the rules.

Charles found his friend, Penny Possum, lying on the grass playing dead. Penny always played dead whenever she felt threatened. The strategy had gotten her through Scary School alive thus far. She had short black hair that hung across her cheeks, and her eyes were so large, she could see in the dark.

Charles nudged Penny and said, "It's okay. The dragons are friendly."

With Charles's assurance, Penny sprang up. She put on her superlarge sunglasses to cover her superlarge eyes.

"Want to ride on the dragon with me?" Charles asked.

Penny nodded.

She'd gone through three years of Scary School without ever speaking a word to anyone. Last year, Charles Nukid tried to save her life by urging her not to read Dr. Dragonbreath's Rule Number Five. Penny gave Charles a piece of candy the next day as a thank-you. Charles didn't understand why she was giving him the candy, so he brought her a piece of candy in return. Because Penny wouldn't speak, they kept giving each other a piece of candy every day— neither knowing why they were doing it.

By the time Charles and Penny were ready to find their dragon, they were shocked to see that every dragon had already been taken. There was only one dragon left—the dragon everyone else was too afraid to ride.

Dr. Dragonbreath.

Charles was happy that he would get to spend time with Dr. Dragonbreath, whom he very much missed having as a teacher. He took Penny's hand and pulled her toward Dr. Dragonbreath, but Penny started shaking her head and backing away.

"Don't worry," said Charles. "Dr. Dragonbreath is my friend. He won't hurt us."

Dr. Dragonbreath was not Charles Nukid's friend. Charles annoyed Dr. Dragonbreath like no other because he followed every rule to the letter, so there was never any hope of making a meal out of him.

Charles and Penny took a seat on Dr. Dragonbreath's back. Dr. Dragonbreath rolled his eyes when he saw who it was.

"Hi, Dr. Dragonbreath!" said Charles. "How's class going so far?"

"Dreadful," Dr. Dragonbreath replied with a snarl. "Four kids followed Rule Number Five, so I have to show up every day and teach them. I was *so* looking forward to a paid vacation."

The lead dragon roared, blowing a stream of fire into the air, signaling the armada of dragons to take to the sky. The journey to the Monster King was under way.

Charles held on tight to the reins attached to Dr. Dragonbreath's head, and Penny wrapped her arms tight around Charles's waist. His heart skipped a beat. He had to take several deep breaths to slow it down.

As Charles soared over the ocean on the back of his favorite teacher with his best friend behind him, resting her head on his shoulder, he thought this was the happiest he could possibly be.

In this ghost's opinion, Charles liked Penny a bit more than as a friend, but he would never admit that to me, so I won't put words in his mouth.

As the flight continued, Penny noticed that the rushing wind was making a mess of Charles's stiff hair. She enjoyed putting each hair back in place.

Charles looked to his left and saw Ms. Fangs flying next to him. She had turned herself into a bat and seemed to be struggling to keep up with the swift dragons. To his right he saw Fritz (who always wore swim goggles) and Tanya Tarantula riding together. Tanya had six of her eight legs wrapped around Fritz, who was shaking with fear that Tanya might bite him at any moment. There will be more about Fritz soon.

After several hours, the flying dragons reached the edge of Monster Forest in Albania. The kids' imaginations ran wild thinking of all the different kinds of monsters lurking beneath the treetops.

Soon, they reached a hill where a great castle stood. Thousands of monsters were standing on the hill, cheering and roaring. There were balloons everywhere, bands playing, and a sign that read:

Welcome, Champions of Scary School!

Fireworks zipped past the flying dragons and exploded in the sky.

The students waved and the dragons blew fire in

the exhilaration of the moment.

Unfortunately, everyone was so distracted by the deafening boom of the fireworks, they did not notice Penny Possum screaming.

One of the fireworks had clipped Dr. Dragonbreath's wing. The impact caused him to jerk backward, sending Charles Nukid flying off his back. Penny tried to reach for him, but it was too late.

Charles Nukid was plummeting to certain death.

10

Don't Mess with Bearodactyls

Dr. Dragonbreath landed in the great courtyard at the entrance of Monster Castle. Penny hopped off him and ran to Principal Headcrusher.

Not one for words, Penny tried pantomiming what had happened. She did spinning jumping jacks trying to illustrate the fireworks, flapped her arms to mimic Dr. Dragonbreath, and even fell backward to show Charles's tragic fall. Principal Headcrusher had no idea what any of it meant.

"Penny, there will be plenty of time for dancing later. Now go stand with your class."

Penny groaned and realized she had no choice but to speak.

"CHARLES NUKID FELL!" Penny spoke as softly as she could, but because she had been holding her voice inside for the last six months, it shot forth like a wrecking ball, knocking over the first several rows of monsters in the audience. The monsters thought it was part of the show and cheered.

Principal Headcrusher looked around to confirm Penny's statement.

"Well," said Principal Headcrusher, "there's nothing we can do. Charles either died from the fall or, if he somehow survived that, the forest monsters will have eaten him by now."

Hearing this, Penny started crying.

"Yes, it's very sad," said Principal Headcrusher, patting Penny on the head. Her giant hands hurt more than they comforted. "Just try to be happy for all the kids who survived the journey. I was expecting far more fatalities."

That didn't help. Penny cried even harder.

Principal Headcrusher was probably the worst person in the world at comforting sad children, but she tried. "Perhaps I was too pessimistic," Principal

Headcrusher said, trying her best to make Penny feel
better. "There's no reason to give up hope just yet."

Penny perked up.

"I'm not saying that Charles is definitely dead. All
I'm saying is that there is absolutely no chance he is
still alive. Does that make you feel better?"

Penny went right back to sobbing.

Charles Nukid opened his eyes. He expected to see clouds and angels all around him since he had so diligently followed the rules his whole life.

Instead, he saw sharp tree branches and three very strange creatures staring him in the face.

It was then that Charles realized he was not dead. At least, not for the moment.

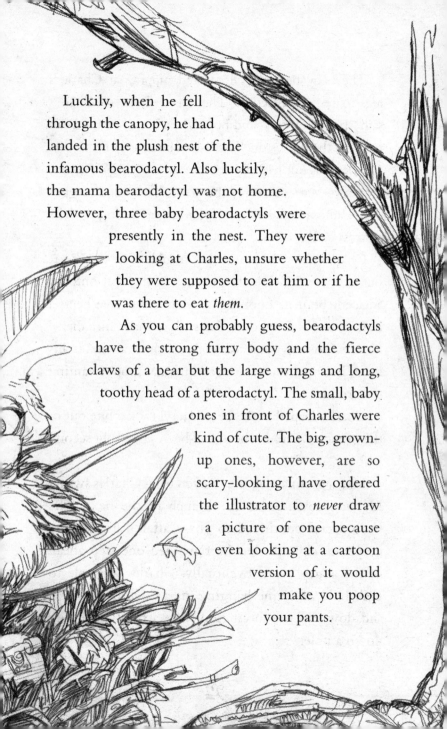

Luckily, when he fell through the canopy, he had landed in the plush nest of the infamous bearodactyl. Also luckily, the mama bearodactyl was not home. However, three baby bearodactyls were presently in the nest. They were looking at Charles, unsure whether they were supposed to eat him or if he was there to eat *them*.

As you can probably guess, bearodactyls have the strong furry body and the fierce claws of a bear but the large wings and long, toothy head of a pterodactyl. The small, baby ones in front of Charles were kind of cute. The big, grown-up ones, however, are so scary-looking I have ordered the illustrator to *never* draw a picture of one because even looking at a cartoon version of it would make you poop your pants.

The baby bearodactyls started nipping at Charles's legs to test his reaction. Their teeth hurt, so Charles said "Bad Monster," and bopped each one on the beak to teach them a lesson. The babies became nervous that Charles was not friendly and started crowing an alarm.

They were answered by a much louder, deeper crow. The mama bearodactyl was responding to their distress call!

Charles knew he was in big trouble if he didn't get out of there fast. He climbed out of the nest onto an adjacent branch. Looking at what must have been a hundred-foot drop to the forest floor made him dizzy. He tried to map out a course down the branches in his head, but then the bearodactyl mama came streaming toward him.

Charles leaped as the bearodactyl took a bite out of the branch where his head had been just a split second before.

Like a gymnast on the uneven bars, Charles swung his way down from one branch to the next. The bearodactyl continued to chase after him, making desperate chomps, but he remained one step ahead of the angry beast. Eventually, Charles was able to grab hold of a vine hanging off a thick branch. He slid down to the forest floor like a fireman sliding down a pole.

The bearodactyl shrieked one last time, but didn't want to follow him to the ground to finish him off.

If the ten-foot bearodactyl was scared of the forest floor, Charles could only imagine what horrors awaited him.

The Scary School students had taken their seats on bleachers set up in the courtyard facing the crowd of monsters. Tanya Tarantula searched the crowd for her parents, but saw no giant tarantulas. She guessed they must still be creatures of solitude and would hate being among a large crowd.

The Monster King was about to make his grand entrance. Horns widened, drums blasted, and eyes rolled. No wait, I mixed those up. Horns blasted, drums rolled, and eyes widened. Yes, that's much better.

The front doors of the castle swung open, and King Zog the Monster King entered the courtyard to waves of applause. Every student stood and cheered when they saw King Zog. It was a sight that few humans had seen.

The Monster King walked proudly to the podium. He had grown much larger since becoming king. His toadlike head had almost tripled in size. His walrus body had become fatter, his scorpion tail was frighteningly long, and his horse legs weren't even visible.

That was because he was wearing a long robe, sewn out of several terrifying creatures, that draped to the ground and trailed behind him.

His crown was made out of fanged animal skulls.

A gust of wind blew past King Zog, and the Scary School students picked up his pleasant scent of fresh mint leaves in a shady pine forest.

He spoke to the crowd: "Greetings, monsters and guests. It is a pleasure to have you all here. I am King Zog, bringer of order, manners, and, above all, tolerance to Monster Kingdom. Yes, these days we monsters can tolerate just about anything. The only things we cannot tolerate are disorder, bad manners, and intolerance. Scary School proved a worthy opponent to all other Scary schools, and it is my honor to hand out several awards to the most outstanding performers. First is Larry Ledfoot, who I am pleased to award with the Most Valuable Kickball Player trophy."

The Scary School students cheered as Larry Ledfoot stood up and plodded his way over to the Monster King. Larry was a sixth grader in King Khufu's class whose feet were made of heavy stone after an unfortunate incident with Ms. Medusa.

Larry had great difficulty taking just one step with his heavy stone feet, much less walking across a long courtyard. It took about ten minutes for Larry to walk just twenty steps to the Monster King to accept his trophy.

"Congratulations, Larry," the Monster King exclaimed, handing him a kickball trophy. "You have brought honor to your puny species."

"Darn right I did!" Larry proclaimed. "I am the greatest! I stand like a statue and kick like a mule!"

"Young man," Zog growled, drooling with anger, "your manners are an abomination. That was the ideal time to say a simple thank-you, and you failed. When you are in my kingdom, you must obey *my* rules. Guards! Punish him!"

Three very scary-looking monster guards with the heads of hyenas and the claws of raptors surged toward Larry at top speed.

Fortunately, Larry had experience defending himself from monsters and knew just what to do. He fell on his back with his stone feet raised into the air. The first monster guard leaped upon him and was about to tear him to shreds, but Larry kicked out with his stony feet and hit the guard square in the chest. The guard flew across the courtyard, squealing in shock. It hit the wall of the castle and slid down onto a spire.

The second and third guards attacked from opposite sides. Thinking fast, Larry kicked out in a dramatic splits position, sending one of the guards flying into

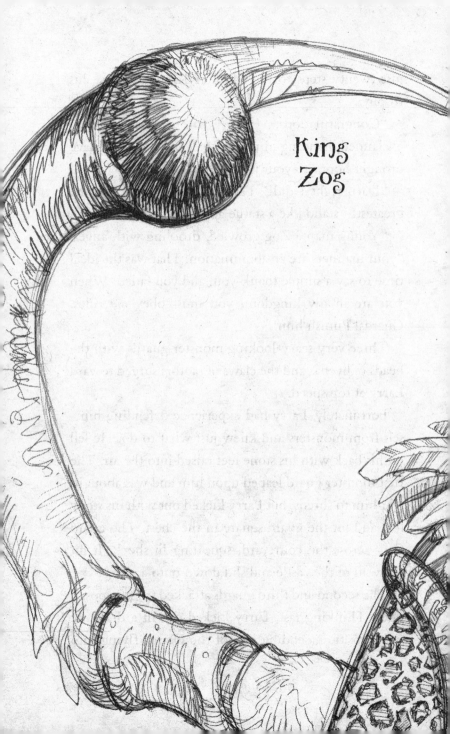

King
Zog

the monster crowd. The other flew so far in the other direction, it landed deep in Monster Forest.

The monsters were so enthralled, they cheered their hearts out as Larry sprang up and bowed to them.

"Thank you! Thank you very much!" Larry exalted, bowing to each part of the crowd.

"Well, better late than never, I suppose," said King Zog, shrugging his walrus shoulders. "You finally said thank you, so you are pardoned. Well done."

Back in Monster Forest, Charles Nukid stealthily . . .

Actually, I think this is a good place to end the chapter. It will give you a chance to grab a spare pair of underwear. You may need them—things can get pretty scary in Monster Forest.

11
The Monster Princess

Back in Monster Forest, Charles Nukid stealth-ily made his way through the trees, moving from one hiding spot to the next, kneeling behind rocks, ducking behind bushes, and diving into leaf piles.

As he was falling through the air, he had seen Monster Castle and made a mental note of where it was. He proceeded in that general direction. If he could get back to his classmates with only a couple limbs missing, he'd call the journey a resounding success.

There were many scary noises echoing and many

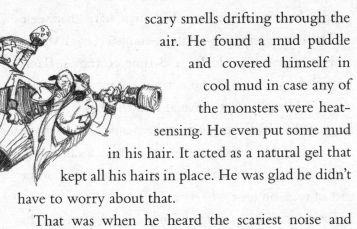

scary smells drifting through the air. He found a mud puddle and covered himself in cool mud in case any of the monsters were heat-sensing. He even put some mud in his hair. It acted as a natural gel that kept all his hairs in place. He was glad he didn't have to worry about that.

That was when he heard the scariest noise and smelled the scariest smell so far.

It was as if a garbage truck filled with rotten eggs was headed straight toward him. He heard a chorus of howls, grunts, and roars over the unmistakable sound of screaming.

Charles quickly dived into an old log as the source of the noise made its way into the clearing. It was a

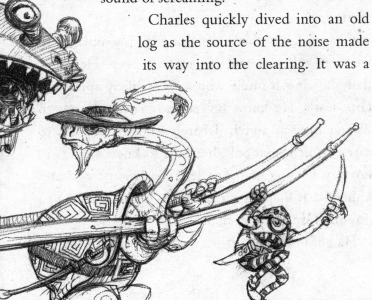

gang of hideous creatures unlike any Charles had seen.

These were monster-pirates—monsters of all shapes and sizes wearing colorful, old-time costumes, flamboyant hats, earrings, nose rings, snout rings, horn rings, and tusk rings. Several had the heads of wild hogs. Some had the heads of serpents. Others were unrecognizable mixtures of jaws, fur, and snouts. They all carried swords and they were dragging some sort of cage on four wheels.

Inside it was a monster with the head of a toad. Its teeth were stumpy and misshapen and it was wearing a lavish red-and-pink gown. Luxurious golden hair hung down to its waist. On top of its head it wore a tiara. "Help! Help!" shouted the caged creature. The monster-pirates just laughed and continued on their way.

Charles knew the smart thing to do would be to let them roll past and not make a peep. He knew that showing himself would most likely spell certain death. He knew he had no claws or fangs to defend himself and had barely enough muscles to carry a thick textbook, but he also knew there was no way he was going to let those monster-pirates kidnap that helpless girl monster without trying to do something to stop them.

He put his hands against the inside walls of the log

and began rolling it toward the moving caravan. The log settled directly in front of the monster-pirates' path. They came to a grinding halt.

A pig-faced monster yelled, "Horace, move the log. We have to make it to the ship by sundown."

Charles crawled out of the log, still covered in mud. Standing tall, he said as authoritatively as he could, "Don't you move another inch."

The monster-pirates stared at Charles in confusion. One of them said, "What is that?"

"I think it's a pile of mud that learned to talk," another answered.

"Don't be stupid! Mud can't talk!"

"But it smells like mud."

Charles shouted, "I'm not mud!" wiping the mud off his face.

The monster-pirates gasped.

In a voice that sounded like a bad imitation of a British queen, the girl monster in the cage proclaimed, "Aha! I told you a dashing hero would come to my rescue! Please, save me quickly, young hero! Ohhhh, it is so dreadful in this vile cage. This is no way for a princess to be treated!"

"Quiet, you!" grunted the pig-faced monster before turning its attention to Charles. "So, since you're not a pile of mud, what are you then? Do you have a name?"

"My name is Charles Nukid. I'm human."

The monster-pirates gasped again.

"A human!" a serpent-headed pirate hissed. "Oh goody, I was hoping for a snack!"

The pig-faced pirate hit the serpent-headed pirate with a stick. "Don't be so rude. Tell me, human, what business have you in Monster Forest?"

"I came to visit the Monster King with my school. You let that girl go, or I will tell the Monster King what you've done."

The monster-pirates laughed. The pig-faced monster stepped forward.

"Foolish human! I am Pigbeard. Captain of the monster-pirates. The princess is mine! Oh, I get it. You see that she is the most beautiful creature on Earth and you want her for yourself!"

"Um, no, I don't. I just don't think—"

"Then we shall do battle for her! The winner will be awarded the princess's hand in marriage."

"I don't want her hand in marriage. I just want you to—"

The princess piped in, "Yes, Charles! Destroy them in battle! Then I shall be yours!"

This was getting out of hand, but Charles was in too deep to back away. That's when he remembered the one thing that monsters are scared of.

Captain Pigbeard drew his sword and aimed it at Charles. "Young human, you have entertained us greatly. But when I am through with you, it seems we *will* be having that human snack."

The monster-pirates laughed and hollered.

Captain Pigbeard circled the defenseless Charles, then dashed toward him, flailing his sword in the air. Charles rolled to the side and shouted, "Seven!"

The monster-pirates screamed in fright. Charles had remembered his Monster Math lessons with Ms. Stingbottom: What monsters fear most are small numbers.

Pigbeard recovered and made another lunge at Charles, but Charles shouted, "Three!" and Pigbeard fell to the ground in fright.

"Stop it! Stop saying those dreadfully small numbers!"

"One!" Charles shouted, and the rest of the monsters fell to the ground and held one another, shaking.

Charles stood up and boldly walked toward Pigbeard. Pigbeard tried crawling away, but Charles hollered, "Negative five!"

Pigbeard turned white with fear. "No! Not negative numbers! Now who's the monster?"

"Negative twelve," Charles yelled. At that, Pigbeard turned and ran to the safety of his pirate cohorts.

Covering their ears, they retreated into the depths of the forest.

Charles approached the monster princess, who was shaking with fear inside the cage, but also happy to be rid of her captors.

"Ohhh, Charles, you did it! Please, free me from this torturous entrapment."

Charles found a hard rock on the ground and

smashed it against the cage lock, breaking it apart.
As the cage door swung open, the monster princess
jumped right on top of Charles, knocking him to the
ground. She gave Charles a big hug and covered him
with kisses.

She smelled like a barrel of sweaty socks doused in
cod liver oil.

"Thank you, my love! Thank you!" she cooed.

"No problem," said Charles. "But I have to get going. My class is waiting for me."

"Of course, of course. But first we must decide on our wedding date."

"Wedding date? Sorry, but I'm only eleven years old. I can't get married yet."

"I am also eleven! Although in monster years, that makes me quite a bit older. I must admit, I have always had a thing for younger men. I am a quarter cougar, after all."

"I don't know what that means," said Charles desperately. "I just need to go find my friends. They're probably with the Monster King right now."

"The Monster King!" exclaimed the princess. "King Zog is my father. I am Princess Zogette. I'll take you to him in a jiffy."

"Really? Sure!"

"Okay, off we go. But first . . . a wedding date."

"I told you. I can't!"

"But you saved me! And that's a rule of Monster Kingdom."

"A . . . rule?" said Charles nervously.

"Yes. If a female monster's life is saved, she must marry the man who saved it."

"Well . . . if that's a rule, then I guess I have no choice. I always follow the rules."

"Perfect. *Now give me a wedding date!*"

Charles said the first date that came into his head, thinking it was his only hope of getting out of Monster Forest anytime soon. "Fine. Christmas."

"Ooohh, Charles! A Christmas wedding. How romantic! Huzzah!"

Satisfied, Zogette picked up Charles, extending a large set of pink feathery wings. She took off into the air toward Monster Castle, hugging Charles in her arms the entire way.

See, kids, sometimes following the rules too closely can get you into trouble. Don't tell your parents I said that.

Back at the courtyard, a couple more students had miraculously saved themselves from certain death after breaking Zog's rules. I don't have the details for you as I was watching Charles Nukid at the time. Yes, I'm a ghost, but I still can't be two places at once. Yeesh.

When I arrived back at the courtyard, Johnny, Ramon, and Peter were accepting their basketball trophies. Unfortunately, right as King Zog was making his speech, one of Johnny's Sasquatch hairs drifted into the nose of Peter, and Peter released a mighty sneeze. He sneezed so hard, it knocked out one of Ramon's zombie eyeballs.

The crowd became silent and King Zog fumed with anger. "How dare you sneeze during my speech! That's a direct violation of Rule Number Four! Guards! Punish them!"

Three monster guards charged toward the three kids. Ramon the Zombie was so scared his toe popped off. But Johnny, Ramon, and Peter played together as a basketball team. They knew how to run a defense.

The three friends stood back-to-back-to-back. Peter quickly transformed into a werewolf, becoming vicious Peter the Wolf. The three monster guards leaped toward them, their claws ready to strike, but at the last second the three friends ducked out of the way. The monster guards clonked heads and dropped dizzily onto the ground.

Johnny quickly grabbed the feet of the first monster guard. With his incredible Sasquatch strength, he flung him onto the roof of the castle. At the same time, Ramon bit the second guard with his zombie teeth, turning him into a monster-zombie. The monster-zombie stomped off in search of brains.

The monster crowd was in shock that the Scary School students were again dispatching the ferocious guards.

Peter the Wolf was tussling on the ground with the

third monster guard, each one gnashing at the other. Johnny and Ramon rushed over to help their friend, but before they got there, King Zog's sticky tongue shot out of his mouth, stuck to the guard's face, and pulled him to his side.

"He is my last guard," King Zog explained. "I need to keep at least one. I pardon each of you. You are worthy members of the monster community. Just don't sneeze, burp, hiccup, or—"

Peter started coughing up a hairball.

". . . *cough* when another monster is speaking."

"Sorry," said Peter the Wolf, changing back into regular Peter. "When you got a hairball, you got a hairball."

At that moment, Princess Zogette and Charles Nukid swept down from the sky and landed in the courtyard.

Charles squirmed away from Zogette's strong arm-lock and tried his best to wipe off her odor.

Penny Possum was so happy Charles had made it back safely that she ran up and hugged him, not caring that he smelled like a pigpen that hadn't been cleaned in months.

Zogette did not like that one bit. She pushed Penny away, grunting, "Back off! He's *mine*."

Penny looked confused. Charles didn't know how

to explain what had happened.

King Zog barged his way in between Charles and Zogette. "What are you doing back here, my disobedient daughter?" Zog bellowed. "I ordered you to marry Captain Pigbeard."

"But Father, I told you I don't want to marry him!"

"And I told you that your marriage to Captain Pigbeard is vital. It's the only way to end a thousand years of war between Monster Kingdom and the monster-pirates. Now you may have ruined it!"

"I care not for politics. All I care about is being with my new fiancé, Charles."

"Who the devil is Charles?!"

Zogette pulled Charles next to her, squeezing him so tight he could barely breathe.

"*This* is Charles. He freed me from Captain Pigbeard and defeated the monster-pirates in battle. We are to be married on Christmas Day."

"Look, Princess," said King Zog, through a forced smile. "I'm not good with human ages, but he looks far too young. How old are you, Charles?"

"I'm eleven," said Charles, still being squeezed and barely able to get the words out.

Princess
Zogette

Every monster shuddered at the mention of Charles's small-numbered age.

"The same as me," said Zogette.

"But in monster years, you're twice as old, Zogette. Enough of this nonsense! Simply say thank you to the human, and we shall send you back to Captain Pigbeard at once."

"No, Father. I am going to be with Charles and we are going to be happy for ever and ever and ever."

Zogette went *pfththth* in Zog's face with her long, sticky tongue.

The monster crowd stared with their mouths agape. King Zog seemed to be holding in a violent outburst with all of his strength.

"And what say you of this, young Charles?" the king asked through gritted teeth.

"I don't even like her," Charles replied.

"Of course not," Zogette crowed. "He doesn't just *like* me. He *adores* me."

"Young man," said King Zog, "Rule Number Five of our land is that you must *never* take anything from another monster without asking. If you take my daughter, you will be taking what rightfully belongs to Captain Pigbeard. Plus, you will be taking my daughter from me without receiving my permission. That means that all of the monster-pirates and all of my monster armies will have no choice but to reclaim what is ours. Tell me, are you prepared to go to war for the hand of Zogette?"

"I—"

"*He is!*" Zogette proclaimed.

King Zog let out a bloodcurdling roar of anger. Then he leaped toward Charles with his scorpion

stinger aimed right at his heart. In the nick of time, Zogette lifted Charles into the air, hovering above the courtyard. King Zog shot out his tongue, but Zogette grasped it before it could stick to them. With monstrous strength, she began swinging her father in circles by his tongue!

When she released her grip, King Zog went flying into the monster crowd, squashing several onlookers. More furious than ever, King Zog commanded, "Monsters! Attack the humans!"

The thousands of monsters on the hillside obeyed their king and roared in unison. They began charging up the hill and climbing the castle walls. The Scary School students were still gathered on the bleachers, not sure what they were supposed to do.

Luckily for them, the dragon-students from Firecrest were returning from their feeding. They blew a wall of fire around the perimeter of the courtyard, temporarily holding back the monster onslaught.

The dragons landed in the courtyard. The students quickly jumped onto their backs. As the dragons took flight, several flying monsters gave chase, but the sleek dragons were much faster than the clunky winged monsters. The students were carried to safety and thankful to have escaped.

Zogette, supporting Charles on her spiky back, held

on to the tail of Dr. Dragonbreath all the way back to Scary School.

When everyone arrived back at school, Charles tumbled off Zogette and ran over to Penny. He noticed that she'd been crying.

"I'm sorry," said Charles sadly. "Zogette told me it was a rule that I had to marry her. But I don't want to. I just wanted her to help me out of the forest."

Penny looked at him like she had a lot to say, but she refused to utter a word for fear that what came out of her mouth might be so powerful, it would blow all of Charles's hair off. I'm guessing what she might have said is: "You were gone for less than an hour, and when you came back, you were engaged to a hideous monster! How could you?"

But instead Penny turned her back on Charles and stomped away.

Charles could only hope that their friendship wasn't over.

Principal Headcrusher stood at the front entrance and made an announcement:

"There is no doubt that the monsters will be coming to retrieve Princess Zogette from Charles. But we must remember that the students and teachers of Scary School are a family. An attack on one of us is an attack on all of us. When the monsters arrive, we must be ready to fight for the love Charles has for his monster bride."

"But I don't even like her!" Charles exclaimed. Nobody heard him, however, because the cheers of support from the students and teachers were so deafening.

12

Fritz vs. the Loch Ness Monster

Fritz was a member of Mr. Grump's sixth-grade class. He wore swimming goggles all day every day.

The reason he wore swimming goggles was simple. He had perfect vision. In fact, he could easily read street signs a whole block away. He was very valuable during car rides. However, he noticed that whenever he went swimming in a pool, his vision became blurry.

Since seventy percent of the Earth is covered in water, Fritz did not like the idea that he only had perfect vision on thirty percent of Earth's surface. By wearing swim goggles all the time, he was guaranteed

Fritz

to have perfect vision no matter where he was on the planet.

Fred had straight, orangish brown hair that hung over his head like wisps of straw on a scarecrow. Thirty percent of his face was covered in freckles and seventy percent was clear skin.

He had large ears, but they didn't work as well as his eyes.

The defining moment of Fritz's life happened when he was five years old. His parents had built a pool in the backyard. The only problem was, Fritz didn't know how to swim. His parents had spent all their money building the pool and had none left to pay for swimming lessons. So, they decided to throw Fritz into the pool with all his clothes on. They figured if he wanted to live, he'd teach himself how to swim.

As Fritz sank to the bottom of the pool, he was very upset that everything around him became blurry. A moment later, he realized that if he didn't do *something* soon, he was going to drown.

He made the decision that he did not want to drown and began to furiously flail his arms and legs. He discovered that moving his arms and legs in a synchronous motion caused him to rise upward.

It's amazing how fast you can teach yourself

something when you will die in thirty seconds if you choose not to.

Fritz was apparently a very good self-teacher, for he shot upward through the water with such a burst of speed, he did a double flip in the air and landed in a perfect dive. He continued to swim around the pool at blinding speed, like his little legs were motors and his tiny arms were propellers.

His parents stood there watching with their mouths hanging open.

His father turned to his mother and said, "I think we may have fed him too many fish sticks."

It was mid-October at Scary School.

A heat wave was sweeping through the region, and the students were hard at work on their daily lessons. But they were happier to be inside the air-conditioned classrooms instead of outside in the blazing heat.

Far away in Monster Kingdom, King Zog was hard at work training legions of monsters in the ways of martial arts in preparation for the upcoming assault upon Scary School to retrieve his daughter.

In Mr. Grump's sixth-grade classroom, the forgetful teacher was hard at work trying to remember the names of the kids who were raising their hands so that he could call on one to answer his question.

He pointed to Jason, who always wore a hockey mask, and said, "What's your name?"

"Jason," replied Jason for the third time that day. "The answer is Abraham Lincoln."

By the time Jason had answered the question, Mr. Grump had already forgotten what the question was and had no idea whether Jason was right or not.

Mr. Grump looked around the classroom to see if he could pick up on whether the class thought Jason's answer was right. He noticed that Petunia was nodding her head at him. She often nodded to indicate whether an answer was right or wrong, just so the lesson could move forward.

"That's correct!" exclaimed Mr. Grump.

"Yes!" said Jason. Then he jumped out of his seat, put on his backpack, and bolted out of the classroom.

"Hey. Why did he leave?" asked Mr. Grump.

"Because," said Wendy Crumkin, "you said that whoever could name the tallest president in US history could have the rest of the day off."

"Oh. Why did I say that?"

"Because you said that we were about to have a surprise and none of us wanted to be here for it."

"All right, if you say so," said Mr. Grump. "Only now I can't remember what the surprise is and I'm getting scared myself. Maybe I'll go home too. Do any of you know where my house is?"

The doors burst open and everyone jumped in fright.

"Good afternoon," said Mr. Snakeskin, the school gym teacher.

Mr. Snakeskin had big, bulging muscles all over his body and wore a red-and-blue sweat suit. His hair was chopped in a crew cut. He looked very mad most of the time. He could also remove his skin whenever he wanted and then put it back on because he was half zombie.

"For your big surprise today," Mr. Snakeskin continued, "Principal Headcrusher has ordered that all of you must go swimming in Scary Pool during gym class to beat the heat. Now hop to it! We don't have a second to waste!"

At that, Mr. Snakeskin ripped off his sweat suit. He was only wearing skintight swim trunks underneath. He marched out of the classroom, expecting everyone to follow.

Fritz was ecstatic. His day had finally come! He was terrible at sports and was always the last picked on every team. Because his class had never gone swimming in Scary Pool before, Fritz had never had a chance to show them the one thing he was good at.

Everyone else groaned in aggravation.

Scary Pool was not a place many entered and made it out alive.

Each kid in Mr. Grump's class got into an official Scary School bathing suit. The suits were brightly colored in oranges and yellows so that the wearer stood out in case there was an emergency. Unfortunately, the bright colors also attracted the most dangerous creatures in the pool, but we'll get to that in a moment.

The water of Scary Pool was as black as tar. Nobody could see what lurked within its depths. It was also enormous—the size of a football field. Just swimming one lap looked like it would take the entire gym class period.

Something about the pool seemed vaguely familiar to Mr. Grump, but he couldn't say why.

Bubbles started bubbling up on the surface of the pool. When they popped, growling sounds could be heard. There was definitely something alive in there.

"All right," said Mr. Snakeskin. "Who wants to jump in first?"

All the kids shook their heads and backed away. Even Fritz was hesitant. He wanted to show how well he swam, but he didn't want to get eaten in the process.

"No volunteers, eh?" Mr. Snakeskin huffed. "It's

perfectly safe. I'll go in first to show you."

Mr. Snakeskin bent his knees on the diving board, held the pose for a few seconds, then did a perfect dive into the water.

He disappeared beneath the surface. After several moments, Mr. Snakeskin had still not come back up. Each second that Mr. Snakeskin didn't appear felt like an hour.

Then, dozens of bubbles began popping up on the water's surface. Each time a bubble popped, they could hear the gurgled voice of Mr. Snakeskin shouting, "Help! . . . Help! . . . Help!"

The class turned to the one they relied on in situations like this—Fred, the boy without fear. Fred had once pulled twenty-two students and a teacher to safety from a fire in science class. Of course, the only one he didn't save was yours truly, but I'm learning to forgive him. A little.

This time Fred shrugged his shoulders and said,

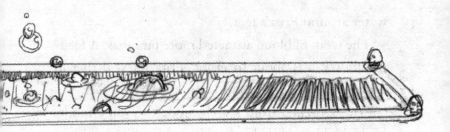

"Don't look at *me*. I don't swim well at all."

The class started to panic. Fritz knew he was the only one who could save the gym teacher. He tightened his swim goggles and stepped to the front of the pool.

"What do you think you're doing?" Lindsey shouted.

Fritz declared, "I'm doing . . . what I was born to do."

As Fritz dived into the water, the students screamed in terror.

Beneath the surface, the water was murky, but Fritz's goggles allowed him to see just well enough to navigate.

He swam toward the middle of the pool, where the bubbles had surfaced. Something started nipping at Fred's toes. He turned his head and saw several piranhas trying to bite them, like his toes were little chicken nuggets. The piranhas' teeth were razor sharp, and drops of blood began seeping into the water around Fritz's feet.

The scent of blood attracted more piranhas. A feeding frenzy was about to erupt. Fritz guessed that in about five seconds, he would no longer have feet.

Fritz switched from search mode to escape mode. He kicked his legs as hard as he could, taking off like a bullet through the water. The swift piranhas remained hot on his tail, and Fritz was running out of air.

He surged upward and went airborne, sucking in as much air as he could. The piranhas were unrelenting.

They followed him out of the water, creating an arch of hungry flying fish.

The class cheered when Fritz burst from the water. But as soon as the piranhas leaped out of the water after him, they screamed. They were certain Fritz was a goner.

Back in the water, Fritz saw a light shining through the murk. He swam toward it with the piranhas in pursuit.

When he swam through the light, the scenery changed drastically. He was no longer in dark, murky water. Now the water was a crystal-clear blue. The piranhas halted behind him, as if blocked by an invisible wall. Before him was a beautiful, vibrant coral reef.

There were colorful clown fish, sinuous jellyfish, concealed eels, a carnival of barnacles, and cuddly cuttlefish generating dynamic displays of luminous light. (That, my dear readers, is called flowery writing. For your sake, I don't do it often, but I couldn't resist.)

There was still no sign of Mr. Snakeskin, and only one place Fritz hadn't looked. He took a deep breath of air from the surface, then swam into an ominous underwater cave.

Fritz's perfect vision was of no use in the pitch-black cave. He had to rely on his imperfect ears. Then—a sound in the darkness! It was the blubbering voice of Mr. Snakeskin calling for help. Fritz just needed some sort of light.

Then Fritz felt something slimy on his leg. A cuttlefish! Fritz grabbed hold of the football-sized mollusk. The cuttlefish created its own bioluminescence. When Fritz squeezed the cuttlefish, the cave lit up like a multicolored disco ball.

Fortunately, Fritz was able to spot Mr. Snakeskin. Unfortunately, Mr. Snakeskin was grasped in the claws of a hundred-foot sea monster with the head of a barracuda.

The light drew the attention of the sea monster. It lunged toward Fritz with its eighty-foot neck, but Fritz took off like a bumblebee, making dizzying circles around the monster's head. The sea monster continued snapping, but Fritz was so fast it was like trying to catch a fly with your bare hands.

Fritz squeezed the cuttlefish on and off, creating a strobe effect in the dark cave, further confusing the monster. It grew weary and released its grip on Mr. Snakeskin. Fritz seized the opportunity and dashed toward him. Mr. Snakeskin deftly grabbed on to Fritz's shoulder as he swam by.

Fritz churned his mighty legs and dragged Mr. Snakeskin out of the cave like a speedy tugboat. The monster roared in frustration, and the roar created an underwater wave that pushed Fritz ahead.

Fritz and Mr. Snakeskin surfaced, riding a thirty-foot tidal wave all the way back to shore. The class was cheering like crazy.

Mr. Grump pulled Fritz and Mr. Snakeskin onto land with his brawny trunk. Fritz breathed the sweet, sweet air as deeply as he could.

Mr. Snakeskin immediately bounded up and shook the water off himself. Then he opened his skull, took out his brain, and wrung the water out like a sponge. As he placed his brain back in his head, he said to the class, "See? It's perfectly safe!"

All of a sudden, the hundred-foot sea monster rose out of the water.

"Kids," Mr. Snakeskin declared, "say hello to Nessie, the Loch Ness Monster. It gets very cold in Scotland, so Scary Pool is her home for fall and winter."

"Hi, Nessie," said the class.

The monster let out a bloodcurdling roar, which was her way of saying hello back.

"Mr. Snakeskin, how did you survive underwater for so long?" asked Frank, which is pronounced "Rachel."

"I'm half zombie. I survived hundreds of years buried underground. A few minutes underwater is

131

no big deal. And I must apologize to all of you. The other side of the pool is the not-so-certain-death area. This side of the pool is the certain-death area. I always get them confused."

The students smacked their hands on their foreheads.

For the remainder of gym, Mr. Grump's students went swimming in the not-so-certain-death area. As long as Fritz was in the water, every kid felt safe. Mr. Grump even joined the fun and sprayed water with his trunk. It was the best gym class ever, thanks to Fritz.

After that day, Fritz was no longer viewed as the worst athlete in the class. He was now considered the *best* athlete in the class. Instead of being picked last on every team, he was always picked first.

Unfortunately, Fritz's talents did not extend to land sports, and the teams that chose him first always lost.

13

A Monstrous Halloween

After a revoltingly delicious lunch of peanut butter and jellyfish, scrambled vulture eggs, and broccoli cake, the students made their way to Petrified Pavilion for the special Halloween assembly.

As they took their seats, Principal Headcrusher took the stage and raised her enormous hands to her mouth.

"Happy Halloween," Principal Headcrusher announced, sounding loud even to the students with their ears plugged. "As you are aware, we have no choice but to watch the goblins' Halloween play before we move on to more important matters. I am aware there is very little chance of this happening, but please *try* to enjoy the goblins' production of *Little Red Riding Hood*."

At this point, the goblins did their performance of *Little Red Riding Hood*, but this year it was *so* awful and poorly executed, I couldn't bring myself to force you to read about it. I'm just not that mean. If you *really* want to read about what happened though, you can head over to my website, ScarySchool.com. Click on the link near Goblin Hill and you can read to your heart's content, but don't say I didn't warn you.

For now I'll tell you that not a single person clapped, and the goblins didn't even deserve that much applause.

As the curtain closed on them, Principal Head-crusher took the stage and said, "Yikes! And I thought *last* year was bad when they destroyed the playground! Now to the important matter at hand. I have invited a special guest who will give us some valuable tips on how we can survive the upcoming monster attack on the school. Please welcome Ms. Stingbottom!"

Every kid in the school stood up and cheered. Ms. Stingbottom was one of their favorite guest teach-ers. She taught basic Monster Math, which, as you remember, Charles Nukid had put to good use in scaring off the monster-pirates.

Ms. Stingbottom stepped up to the podium. She was covered in pink fur from head to foot. She had the head of a lion, the claws of a lobster, and the tail of a stingray. She also wore a very fashionable purple dress that matched her purple purse and purple makeup. All the girls were jealous of her outfit, except for Petunia, of course.

"Awoo-Aloo, my precious students of Scary School!" she exclaimed.

"Awoo-Aloo," the students joyously replied. That made Ms. Stingbottom so happy she did a double backflip.

"I wish I could be here under more cheerful circumstances, but unfortunately I bear only bad news. As a monster, I must admit that members of my species do tend to overreact when they feel they have been insulted. I tried to convince them that you are all very nice children who do not deserve a gruesome death, but I'm afraid I was unsuccessful. Our dragon friends have been tracking their movements, and I feel it is important that you all see this."

Ms. Stingbottom pressed a remote control button, and a giant screen lowered from the ceiling.

"This is live streaming footage of what is occurring

just ten thousand miles away."

A thousand menacing monster-pirate ships filled the screen. The students gasped.

"Yes," Ms. Stingbottom declared, "I fear that one thousand ships are on their way to Scary School even as we speak. The good news is that the monster-pirates are not the world's best navigators. They took off in the wrong direction, which has bought us some time. Nonetheless, they will eventually circle the Earth. I estimate they will arrive here in sixty-five thousand weeks."

All the students did some quick Monster Math in their heads and realized that meant just six human weeks. Everyone looked around nervously, but then Wendy Crumkin raised her hand.

"Yes, Wendy?"

"When they get here, can't we just use Monster Math to scare them away?"

"That is the worst news," Ms. Stingbottom said, shaking her furry lion's head with dozens of pretty ribbons tied to it. "The monsters have all bought . . ." She could barely muster the words and sobbed as she said, "Earplugs!"

The students groaned. Many had been practicing shouting small numbers, but now that seemed all for naught.

"The monsters won't be able to hear anything you say, so you will have to think of a new way to survive the attack. My precious darlings, it is times like this when it is most important to remember what we are fighting for. It is something that most monsters do not even know the meaning of. Love. The love of Charles Nukid and Princess Zogette."

"I don't like her!" Charles shouted from the thick of the crowd.

"Indeed," said Ms. Stingbottom, "their affection has transformed into something quite a bit more than 'like,' and it is the most beautiful thing in the world. Will Charles Nukid and Princess Zogette please join me onstage?"

"Huzzah!" Zogette exclaimed, taking Charles in her arms and flying them down to the stage.

Ms. Stingbottom gazed upon the princess and recoiled.

"Is this the face that launched a thousand ships?" she asked the crowd. "Seriously, is *this* the face? She's hideous even by monster standards. But to each his own, I guess."

Lindsey shouted from the seats, "Hey! Don't judge her by her looks!"

Charles couldn't have been more embarrassed. Princess Zogette was hugging and kissing and pinching him all over.

Ms. Stingbottom continued, "Look upon them, students of Scary School. The purity of their love and devotion is worth defending. It is worth fighting for. It is worth dying for."

Charles decided he had had enough. At that moment, he no longer cared about how much sleep

138

he would lose if he broke a rule. He didn't even care if the princess devoured him in a fit of rage. He was going to break up with her and put an end to this madness.

He turned to give Zogette a piece of his mind, but saw she was holding out a great big present for him.

"Ooohh, Charles," she said, "you are the bravest man in the world. I can never repay you for saving me from the misery of becoming a monster-pirate's bride. Please take this Halloween present as a token of my eternal gratitude."

Charles unwrapped the box. Inside was something so beautiful it left him speechless.

A brand-new, limited edition, Guitar Legend guitar. It looked like it was made of pure gold with sparkling silver trim. The head was in the shape of a thunderbolt. There were signatures all over the face.

"I pulled a few strings, pun intended, and got the guitar signed by all your favorite Monsters of Rock," the princess announced with pride.

Charles examined the signatures and his jaw dropped. There was Deaddie Van Halen, Jack-o'-lantern White, Dave Troll, Shivers Cuomo—just to name a few. If you know who they are, you have great taste in music.

He held the guitar in his arms, still speechless. He looked at Zogette's toady smiling face and couldn't bring himself to break up with her. He meekly said, "Thank you. It's the best present anyone's ever given me." Zogette was so happy, she flicked out her frog tongue and gave Charles a sloppy lick on the face.

"Awww," said the entire crowd, except Penny.

"You see," proclaimed Ms. Stingbottom, "this is what love is all about—a weird toad creature and a skinny human making each other happy. Awoo-Aloo to the both of you."

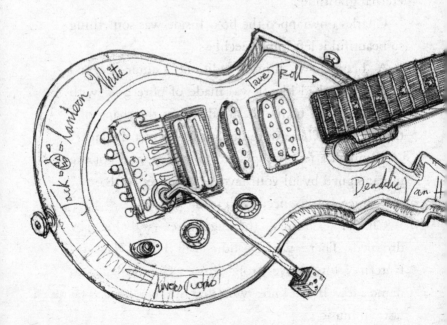

Up in the crowd, Penny Possum's giant eyes were filling with giant tears. Charles noticed and tried to wave to her, but the princess yanked him into her belly and gave him a big, smelly hug.

Later that day, Charles managed to break away from Zogette and went looking for Penny Possum. He found her in her favorite hiding spot between lockers 217 and 218.

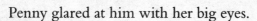

Penny glared at him with her big eyes.

"Penny," he said, "I didn't mean for any of this to happen. I really miss you. You were my best friend. I still want you to be."

He mussed up his perfectly coiffed hair just to make her laugh. Penny's grim expression didn't change.

"Listen," Charles pleaded, "we haven't talked in a long time. Fifty-five and a half days, to be exact. I mean, I know we never talked anyway, but we at least had—"

Before Charles could finish, Penny had keeled over and played dead, telling him without words that the conversation was over.

Charles exhaled deeply as his heart sank. Walking away, he carefully put each hair back in its place.

14 ~
Eddie Bookman Doesn't Exist... Or Does He?

E ddie Bookman is no-doubt-about-it, hundred-percent-guaranteed, certain that he doesn't actually exist. In fact, he is absolutely convinced that he is a fictional character in a fictional book.

Everyone at Scary School thinks he's crazy, but perhaps he's the least crazy of them all.

On a brisk November morning, Eddie was sitting in King Khufu's class. He believed with all his heart that he wasn't *really* there. King Khufu asked everyone to pass forward their homework.

Everyone always did their homework in King Khufu's class because they were scared to death that Khufu would place a horrible curse on them if they failed to. That is exactly the reason why parents pay so much to send their kids to Scary School. Being in constant fear of losing their lives makes the children work harder than they've ever worked. As a result, Scary School produces the smartest, most over-achieving human students in the world.

As soon as King Khufu noticed Eddie's homework was missing, his bandaged limbs froze and he glowered at Eddie with his ancient eyes. He unwrapped the cloth that usually covered his mouth, and the stench of his ancient breath filled the room.

"Mr. Bookman," hissed King Khufu, "where is your homework?"

"I didn't do it," Eddie answered calmly.

"And may I ask why?"

"Because I don't exist."

The class burst into laughter, and even King Khufu chuckled.

"What do you mean you don't exist?"

"I mean I'm a character in a book—and a very weird book at that. Some writer made me up, probably just a few minutes ago. So if that's all I am—the figment of some weird writer's imagination—what is the point of doing homework?"

King Khufu scowled. He was certain Eddie was trying to trick him or confuse him to get out of being cursed. Then he thought of something and snapped his dusty fingers, causing the tip of his thumb to break off. "Tell me—ow, my thumb—

Eddie
Bookman

do you have any proof that you don't exist, Mr. Bookman?"

"Yes, I do."

The class leaned in with interest.

"What do I look like?" Eddie asked.

Everyone in the class looked at one another, not sure of how to answer. Even King Khufu seemed flummoxed. Khufu stammered, "You look like . . . like . . . um . . ."

Eddie had a thick flattop of black hair; pale, freckly skin; and was wearing a green striped shirt with brown shorts and hiking shoes.

"Ah, I know exactly what you look like," said Khufu. "You have a thick flattop of black hair; pale, freckly skin; and you are wearing a green striped shirt with brown shorts and hiking shoes."

"See! Why did it take you so long to answer me? It's because whoever's writing this had no idea what I looked like thirty seconds ago. He just pulled it out of thin air."

"That's ridiculous," said Khufu. "We can all see what you look like."

"But *I* don't even know what I look like," Eddie exclaimed, rising from his chair. "For all I know you could be lying to me, 'cause I've never looked in a mirror!"

Eddie had looked in a mirror that morning and had thought that he looked particularly handsome.

"Okay, never mind," said Eddie. "I did look in a mirror this morning, but I swear I didn't know that until two seconds ago."

Once again the class broke out into laughter. Even Tanya Tarantula rolled onto her back and wiggled her fangs at Eddie's nuttiness. Princess Zogette exclaimed, "You aren't anywhere near as handsome as my Charles!" then she flew across the room and gave Charles a big kiss on the cheek. The slobber stuck to his face for the rest of the day.

"It's a good try, Eddie," said Khufu. "But I'm afraid I have no choice but to curse you for not doing your homework."

"Whatever," said Eddie. "I think I'm already cursed."

By lunchtime, word had spread fast about Eddie's behavior in class.

As he walked through the lunch hall, everyone was pointing and laughing at him. Even the zombie waiters were laughing so hard that their jaws fell off. The school had been desperately searching for something to laugh about to take their minds off the thousands of karate monsters on their way to attack them.

Lebok, a big, mean troll in the sixth grade, walked up to Eddie and socked him in the arm.

"Ow," said Eddie. "Why'd you do that?"

"Hey, if you no exist, you should no have hurt, right?"

Lebok started laughing, and everyone in the lunch hall laughed along with him. Even dumb trolls were scoring points off Eddie.

Then Eddie walked by a table of fifth-grade girls. They began throwing their food at him, creating a disgusting mess all over his clothes.

"Why'd you do that?" Eddie asked them.

"What do you care? If you don't exist, then it's impossible to look stupid, right?"

That was the last straw. Eddie jumped onto a table-top and screamed, "I AM JUST A CHARACTER IN A BOOK! AND GUESS WHAT? ALL OF YOU PROBABLY ARE TOO! As soon as I find a way to prove it, I'll show you!"

Then *all* the kids in the lunch hall started throwing their food at poor Eddie. None of them felt bad about it, because if Eddie didn't exist, that meant he didn't have any feelings.

He could only wonder why the writer of this story disliked him so much that he should have to go through all this anguish.

While Eddie was eating all by himself, three sisters named Sarah, Lily, and Mia, each born one year apart and all with long black hair, approached Eddie and gave him some advice.

"If what you say is true," said Sarah, "then the one to talk to is Derek the Ghost."

Lily piped in, "He's writing a book about Scary School, so if you really are just a character in a book, he would have created you."

Mia added, "I just saw him floating around by the quicksand box. If you hurry, you might catch him before he goes into his haunted house."

Sarah, Lily, and Mia thought Eddie's theory might be true because, aside from Petunia, they were the only kids at Scary School who had read the first Scary School book.

"Thanks," said Eddie to the sisters. "I'll do that."

Eddie abandoned his lunch and ran as fast as he could to the quicksand box. I was sitting there building a castle. One of the advantages of being a ghost is that I have no weight, so I couldn't sink into the quicksand.

"Hey, are you Derek the Ghost?" Eddie asked.

"Yes," I said.

"So . . ." Eddie hesitated, knowing the question he wanted to ask, but unsure if he actually wanted to hear the answer. "Do I . . . I mean . . . am I just a character in your book?"

"Of course you are," I said. "I float around writing about everything and everyone at the school. That's my job. I certainly wouldn't leave you out."

"I know *that*. But I mean, do I actually exist or did you just make me up?"

I floated out of the sandbox and hovered next to Eddie.

"Listen," I said, "you already seem sure that you don't exist, so why are you even asking me?"

"You're right," he said. "I am sure. So why did you curse me to be the only kid at the school who realizes it?"

"To be honest, I thought you'd enjoy your life more if you knew the big secret."

"Enjoy it? I'm *miserable* because nobody believes me."

"Ah, so you want proof to show the other kids."

"Yes! Exactly. That would be fantastic."

"There's only one way to prove your nonexistence for a fact."

I pointed to a glowing blue circle on the ground.

"You have a choice. You can either go on living your life from this point forward with the sole knowledge that you don't actually exist. Or, you can gather all the kids out here and stand on that circle. Then, you'll have your proof."

"Great!" said Eddie. "I'll get the kids out here right away."

Eddie ran back into the lunch hall and brought everyone out to the playground. He had promised he had proof that he was right and they were wrong.

The students and teachers all watched intently as Eddie walked toward the glowing blue circle on the ground. Grinning with excitement, he stepped toward the circle. Everyone held their breath.

As soon as he stepped inside the circle . . . he was gone. Vanished. Not only from his physical form, but also from everyone's thoughts and memories.

Eddie Bookman had never existed.

The students began asking one another, "Why are we out here?"

"I don't know. Let's go back into the lunch hall."

The students made their way back into the lunch hall, and now none of them could dispute the fact that Eddie Bookman did not exist, because none of them had ever heard of him.

Eddie Bookman was proven right. Except, he never got the chance to gloat about it because he had never existed.

15

Skeletons in the Closet

As Marvin the ogre wheeled his mop bucket down the hallway, he kept hearing strange noises behind him.

Kids were shouting, "Whoa!", "Yah!", and "Whoops!"

He turned around and noticed a trail of red-tinted mop water that led straight to his bucket. The kids walking down the hallway didn't see the water and were slipping and sliding down the hallway.

Marvin was the Scary School janitor. As such, his mop bucket was usually filled with blood from mopping up the daily carnage.

Marvin was not very smart, even for an ogre. His bottom jaw stuck way out, his teeth seemed to jut in all directions, his nose was flat and twisted, his brow hung over his eyes, and he had lumpy greenish skin on his bald head.

Marvin inspected the bucket and said to himself, "Uh-oh. There's a hole in my bucket."

Marvin scratched his lumpy head for several minutes trying to think of what to do about it.

With what shall I fix it? thought Marvin. I could get some straw, but the straw is too long. I would have to cut it. But with what would I cut it? I know. A blade. But the blade is too dry.

Marvin realized this line of thinking could possibly

go on forever, so he just decided, Ah, the heck with it. I'll get a new bucket.

Marvin went to the supply closet where he kept all his spare buckets. Despite being the Scary School janitor for over ten years, this was the first time he had needed a new bucket. Thus, this was his first time entering the spare-bucket supply closet.

Marvin took out a big ring of keys. He had trouble remembering which key opened the door. Eventually, he opened it, and his big ogre jaw dropped to his chest in fright. He quickly shut the door and relocked it.

Marvin lumbered into Principal Headcrusher's office. She was busy doing paperwork.

"Boss," said Marvin in his slow voice, "skeletons in the closet."

Without looking up, Principal Headcrusher replied, "Yes, Marvin, we all have skeletons in our closets."

"But boss . . . uh . . . skeletons in the closet. Real skeletons. Bones. Buckets. Uhhh . . . bones."

Principal Headcrusher exhaled, realizing Marvin was not going to leave her alone until she saw what the problem was. She followed him to the supply closet, and Marvin opened the door again.

This time, as soon as the door opened, three

skeletons, each no bigger than an eleven-year-old kid, leaped out of the closet into the hallway shouting, "We're free! We're free!" They danced a frenetic skeleton dance. It looked like they were being controlled by bad puppeteers. Their teeth clanked and their bones rattled as they hopped about.

"Who are you three?" inquired Principal Headcrusher.

"I'm Skeletony!"

"I'm Skeletammy!"

"And I'm Skeletommy!"

"Wait a second," said Principal Headcrusher. "Tony Malto, Tammy Gerber, and Tommy Stubbs? You three went missing over five years ago."

"I know," said Skeletony. "We were being chased by the gargoyles and hid in the closet for safety. But it was locked from the outside and nobody heard us banging and calling for help."

"That makes sense," said Principal Headcrusher. "All the doors are soundproof, otherwise it would be very hard to hear your teachers over the screaming."

Skeletammy continued, "Eventually we died and turned into skeletons."

"We learned a very important life lesson about not hiding in strange closets," said Skeletommy.

"Once we became skeletons, we renamed

157

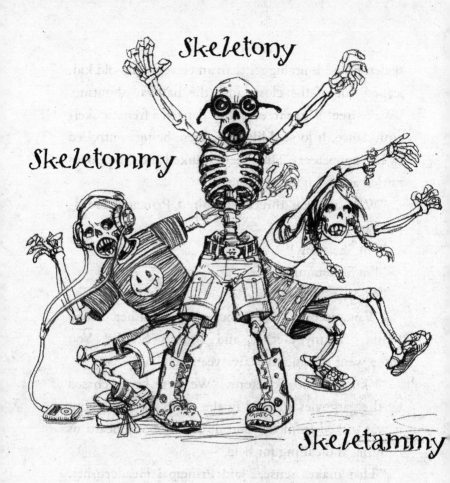

Skeletony

Skeletommy

Skeletammy

ourselves Skeletony, Skeletammy, and Skeletommy," said Skeletony.

"Coming up with those names kept us busy for the last three years," said Skeletommy.

"We didn't always get along, though," said Skeletammy.

"Yeah, we always had a bone to pick with one

another," said Skeletony.

The three skeletons cackled at the joke they were far too proud of.

"Well," said Principal Headcrusher, "you're free to go off into the world and live your skeletal lives now. I'm sure you'll be able to find jobs hanging in high school biology classrooms."

"No!" Skeletammy chattered. "We decided that if we ever got out, we would stay at Scary School and finish our education. Since we're Scary kids now, we get to attend for free, right?"

"Um . . .," said Principal Headcrusher awkwardly. "That *would* be possible. If you were actually Scary kids."

"What?" exclaimed Skeletony. "We're skeletons! What's scarier than that?"

"Everything?" replied Principal Headcrusher.

"That's ridiculous," said Skeletommy. "We'll prove to you right now that we're scary. Come on, guys, let's go scare some kids."

The skeletons went to a classroom, accompanied by Principal Headcrusher.

Oh, and by the way, after Marvin got his new mop bucket from the supply closet, he happily went back to his mopping, and that's where his part in this story comes to an end.

The first classroom the skeletons went to was King Khufu's. The skeletons burst into the room right in the middle of King Khufu's lecture on why cats should be worshipped as gods. They cackled their skeleton laugh and rattled their skeleton bones.

King Khufu and his students stared at them blankly. Not even Steven Kingsley was afraid.

"King Khufu, is this part of the cwass?" asked Cindy Chan.

"No, it isn't," answered Khufu. "I'll handle this." He turned to the three skeletons and hissed, "Who dares disturb the peace of my class?"

Still cackling and rattling their bones, the three skeletons replied, "We're the scary skeletons! Kneel before us in fear!"

Nobody knelt.

"Come on!" the skeletons urged. "We're the living dead!"

"And how long have you been dead for?" asked King Khufu.

"About five years," they replied.

"Five years? Ha! That's hardly dead at all. I've been dead over four thousand, five hundred years. Now, *that's* dead. Begone from here."

The three skeletons hung their bony heads and clopped out of the room, but they weren't ready to give up. Next they burst into Ms. Fangs's fifth-grade class.

It went about the same.

"You've only been dead for five years?" Ms. Fangs laughed. "I've been dead over eight hundred and fifty years. I may not be as dead as King Khufu, but I'm much more dead than you."

They decided to try one last classroom, Mr. Grump's. At least he was still alive. They ran up and down the aisles, but because they no longer had any muscles, they ended up tripping every few strides. The class was laughing at them.

"Stop laughing!" pleaded Skeletammy. "We're not funny. We're scary."

The three skeletons collapsed in a heap, utterly confused and exhausted.

"Sorry, but there's nothing scary about you," said Wendy Crumkin.

"Yeah. You don't have big strong muscles, like me," said Johnny the Sasquatch. Johnny flexed his muscles and roared. Everyone jumped back in fright.

"And you don't have sharp teeth like me," said Peter the Wolf, baring his teeth and snarling, making everyone jump again.

"And I bet your bones don't even come off like mine do," said Ramon the Zombie, ripping off his left

arm, causing
several students
to pass out in shock.

"I don't understand. Haven't skeletons always been considered scary?" asked Skeletommy.

Petunia replied, "Skeletons are only scary when you find them someplace they're not supposed to be. We expect to see skeletons at Scary School, so you're not scary here."

The skeletons realized Petunia was right. They left the room with their skulls hanging low.

"You see?" said Principal Headcrusher. "You're just not as scary as the thought of the ten thousand monsters that will attack the school next month."

The skeletons decided there was no use hanging around somewhere where they weren't appreciated. They ventured off in search of a place that didn't have any zombies, vampires, or mummies.

Eventually they came to a quaint-looking town and peered over a fence to where a young lady was planting flowers in her backyard garden.

When the lady went inside for a drink of water, the

skeletons dived into the soil. When the lady resumed her shoveling, she hit Skeletony in the head with her shovel. When she uncovered the three skeletons grinning at her, she screamed in fright and ran back into the house.

The three skeletons high-fived and exclaimed, "All right! We still got it!"

16
Thanksgiving with the Dark Lord

I t was Thanksgiving break.

All the Scary School students were at home with their families, enjoying what was sure to be their last holiday together. Nobody was expecting to survive the monster attack, which was on schedule to take place in just three weeks.

To mark the occasion, Princess Zogette joined Charles Nukid's family for dinner. I crashed the dinner uninvited just for your sakes, my loyal readers.

Zogette was very excited to participate in the human tradition of Thanksgiving. Her love for

Charles was matched only by her love for food. She couldn't wait for the grandest of human feasting days. Charles's parents, Clarence and Wanda Nukid, were also excited that Zogette would be joining them for Thanksgiving. They were elated that Charles had fallen in love with a real-life princess and they pictured themselves living in a faraway castle with throngs of servants.

One of the rules Charles followed at home was to never speak poorly of another person, so he found himself unable to tell his family that he didn't really like Zogette. The dinner went very well until they brought out the turkey. As the guest of honor, Zogette had the privilege of cutting the first piece, but she thought the whole turkey was being offered to her. She swallowed the entire twenty-pound bird in one gulp.

And so it became a vegetarian Thanksgiving at the Nukid house.

Principal Headcrusher was using the time off to pay a visit to an orphanage in a remote village by the sea. While on vacation, Principal Headcrusher preferred to go by her given name of Meredith Headcrusher.

The orphanage was rumored to house a ten-year-old boy with extraordinary powers named Tim Puzzle.

Meredith thought that his powers could help defeat King Zog's army. But she would need to convince him to attend Scary School first.

When Meredith arrived at the village (driving her car with a special oversized steering wheel to fit her hands), she had a good deal of trouble finding the orphanage because oddly there were no street signs. She ended up circling the streets for hours before finding the building.

Once there, she placed her enormous compact mirror in her enormous hand and finished applying her makeup. Then she placed her hands in her enormous pants pockets so as not to scare anyone as she headed inside the orphanage to meet with the matron.

The matron was a pleasant-looking, plump old woman named Mrs. Green. Mrs. Green was wearing a bright green muumuu

and glared at Meredith with piercing green eyes.

"Hello, I'm Meredith Headcrusher, principal of Scary School."

"Headcrusher?" said Mrs. Green. "That's a rather unfortunate name."

"I'm afraid none of us can choose our birth names, can we?"

"Good point. I have a cousin named Dilbert Pickles. He can't stand pickles."

"Exactly. So, I suppose you're wondering why I'm here."

"No. You actually mentioned in your e-mail that you want Tim Puzzle to attend your school. Is that still the case?"

"Possibly. I need to meet him first."

"Don't get me wrong. I'd be thrilled to be rid of him. But I have to warn you that when we found him, he was living all alone in his parents' house except for two pet frogs. His parents had gone missing, you see. When authorities asked him where his parents were, all he said was, 'They tried to make me eat my vegetables and now they're gone.'"

"Well, his parents must not have cooked vegetables very well. At Scary School, Sue the Amazing Octo-Chef cooks the vegetables so deliciously, the kids eat them like candy."

"Well, we can't all be amazing octo-chefs, now can we? We took Tim in to live with us and as soon as he got here, the other kids started to go missing and the frog population started exploding. Odd, considering there aren't any creeks for miles."

"That *is* odd. You think Tim has been turning the other kids into frogs?"

"I can't prove it, of course. If I brought it up with him, I'm pretty sure he'd do something appalling to me, so I leave bad enough alone. Why do you think I wear this hideous green muumuu? Whenever I'm around him, I ribbit and hop about so that he thinks he's already turned me into a frog."

"That's terrible."

"*That* I can handle. The worst part is the fly eating."

"It sounds like Tim is a real handful for you, but he seems perfect for my school."

"Maybe you aren't catching my drift. There are kids with problems and kids with issues to work through, and every so often, there's a kid like Tim Puzzle. He's just plain evil."

"I'll be the judge of that."

"Don't get me wrong! I would do cartwheels and set off fireworks if you took him off my hands. Just don't say I didn't warn you."

Mrs. Green led Meredith into an ornate room on the top floor of the orphanage. Tim Puzzle sat at an antique wooden desk, typing at a computer. At his feet were the remnants of a turkey carcass on a large plate. Meredith surmised he had just eaten his Thanksgiving dinner all alone in his room.

Mrs. Green whispered to Meredith, "A few weeks ago he demanded to have my room. Obviously I agreed. I'll leave you two alone." Then she ribbited and hopped out the door.

As soon as the door closed, Tim Puzzle turned around in his chair. He wore glasses that were taped together at the bridge, and his two front teeth bucked forward over his bottom lip. His brown hair was parted straight down the middle and curled upward when it reached his ears. He was wearing blue shorts and a pin-striped collared shirt. He looked like that kid in class who you try to copy your notes off of, but when he catches you looking, he tells the teacher.

"Who are you?" Tim Puzzle asked in a high-pitched voice that resonated with menace.

"My name is Principal Meredith Headcrusher. I'm from Scary School."

"Scary School? What's that?"

"It's a school where regular kids study with vampires, werewolves, zombies, trolls—you name it. I'm told you have special talents that might make you a perfect fit."

Tim Puzzle shrank away at those words, as if Meredith had learned a secret he didn't want known.

"I don't know what you're talking about. You have the wrong kid."

"Tim, if you don't mind, I'd like to show you something."

Meredith removed her right hand from her pocket and held it up. Tim's jaw dropped. "Gross! Your hand is as big as me!" he exclaimed.

Meredith smiled, then pulled out a whole watermelon from her purse and crushed it with a gentle squeeze, sending rinds and watermelon juice flying everywhere. Tim loved the display and started bouncing

Tim
Puzzle

in his seat.

"Do it again! Do it again!" he urged.

"Okay. But first you have to show me something you can do."

Tim's face turned sour, realizing she had just tricked him, but he did feel a level of trust with Principal Headcrusher.

He led Meredith to a large chest sitting in the corner of the room and opened it. Inside were at least thirty frogs hopping around.

"You like frogs?" Principal Headcrusher asked.

"Not really," replied Tim. "These were other kids at the orphanage who were mean to me. Two of them were my parents. They tried to make me eat vegetables. Would I have to eat vegetables at Scary School?"

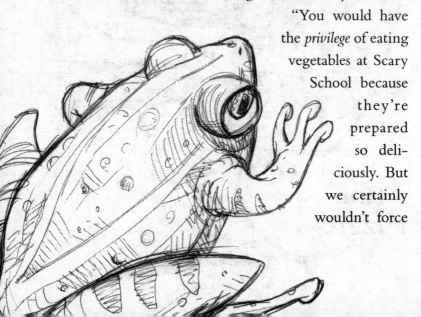

"You would have the *privilege* of eating vegetables at Scary School because they're prepared so deliciously. But we certainly wouldn't force

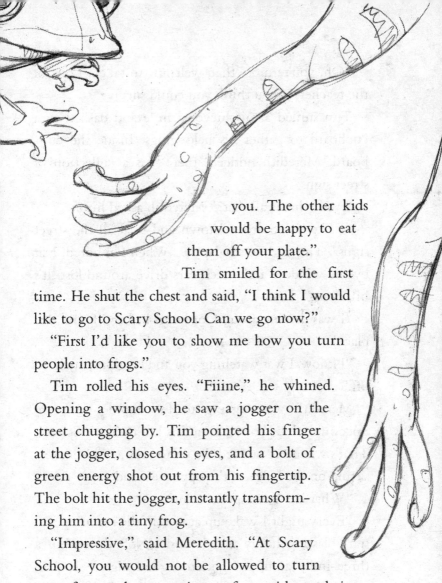

you. The other kids would be happy to eat them off your plate."

Tim smiled for the first time. He shut the chest and said, "I think I would like to go to Scary School. Can we go now?"

"First I'd like you to show me how you turn people into frogs."

Tim rolled his eyes. "Fiiine," he whined. Opening a window, he saw a jogger on the street chugging by. Tim pointed his finger at the jogger, closed his eyes, and a bolt of green energy shot out from his fingertip. The bolt hit the jogger, instantly transforming him into a tiny frog.

"Impressive," said Meredith. "At Scary School, you would not be allowed to turn any of your classmates into a frog without their permission."

"What about the teachers?" Tim asked.

"Oh, you're more than welcome to take on one of the teachers if you think you could survive."

Tim smiled a mischievous smile and dashed to a cupboard to gather his belongings. Inside the cupboard, Meredith noticed, there was a collection of street signs.

"And what is all that?" Meredith asked him.

"I like to go around town and steal all the street signs," Tim said nonchalantly. "When I'm bored, I sit by the window and watch cars drive around lost. It's hilarious."

"I was driving around for hours before I found this place!"

"I know. I was watching you and laughing my head off."

Meredith was starting to feel more and more uncomfortable about taking this kid to Scary School. That's when she noticed the enormous audio speakers sitting on the ledge of the opposite window.

"What are those speakers for?"

"Every night I wake up at two in the morning and start blasting heavy metal music. Nobody within a three-mile radius has gotten a good night's sleep in months."

"Okaaay. You know what," said Meredith. "This isn't going to happen for you."

"What do you mean?" asked Tim, the excitement draining out of him.

"At Scary School, we teach that just because you have the ability to maim and transform and make people's lives miserable, there is almost never a good reason to do it. I'm afraid I made a mistake offering you a place in my school. Have a nice day."

Principal Headcrusher walked back toward the door, leaving Tim stunned and hurt. "Wait!" he screamed. "You let me come to your school, or I will turn you into a frog!"

"Listen, Tim. You are obviously going to be a very powerful wizard one day. Based on your personality, a dark lord, no doubt. I wish you luck with that, but I will not be part of it."

Baring his buckteeth, Tim extended a finger and shot a bolt of green energy at Meredith. Meredith had been expecting this the entire time. She quickly pulled her left hand out of her pocket, in which she was still holding the enormous compact mirror. The bolt of energy bounced off the mirror and reflected back onto Tim.

He was hit right in the chest by his own bolt, instantly transforming him into a tiny green frog.

Tim being turned into a frog created a reverse shock wave of magic that immediately turned all the frogs in the chest back to normal kids. They came spilling out of the chest on top of one another. Even Tim's parents were changed back. The kids hugged Meredith for turning them back into humans.

Tim's parents caught their tiny frog son and placed him in a jar.

When the matron hopped back into the room, she was overjoyed to see all the children had returned. She was even happier that Tim's parents were going to take the young dark lord off her hands.

The Puzzles bought a very nice aquarium for their son, in which he would live out the rest of his days eating bugs and hopping on fake rocks.

He still tried to be the most evil frog he could possibly be. Every night at 2:00 a.m., he croaked as loud as he could.

17
The Thousand-foot Chain

It was early December at Scary School, and the first snow had fallen overnight.

Across the street, at the very peak of Goblin Hill, stood the three best friends—Johnny the Sasquatch, Ramon the Zombie, and Peter the Wolf. Each was holding a snowboard at his side.

Since the monster attack was less than two weeks away, the three friends had decided to make the most of the short time they had left and do something nobody had ever dared to do.

They nodded to one another, then took off down

the hill on their snowboards, heading straight toward the school's front entrance.

Archie the giant squid had felt the vibrations and raised his enormous eye out of the moat to investigate. Archie knew that snowboarding into school was against the rules, so he figured he'd make a quick breakfast of the three friends.

His tentacles rose from the water and he thrashed them wildly in an attempt to catch the boys in his sticky suckers.

But Johnny,

Ramon, and Peter were moving too fast. Ramon slid underneath the suckers, doing a spectacular limbo move; Peter did a twisting jump right straight through a gap in the tentacles; and Johnny deftly ollied off Archie's head, then slid down a tentacle straight into the twisting main hallway.

Archie grumbled with frustration and sank back into the moat.

"Look out!" the three friends yelled as they found themselves speeding like bullets between the rows of lockers.

Students were diving out of the way, but it proved unnecessary as the three snowboarders had jumped over them and were now sliding along the top of the lockers.

Unfortunately, they were fast approaching the hall monitor, Ms. Hydra. She was chatting with Dr. Dragonbreath outside his classroom.

As the snowboarders zoomed past Ms. Hydra, four of her heads were furious and wanted to chase after them.

"Snowboarding in the hallway! I never!" said the first head.

"Let's get 'em!" said the sixth head.

The ninth head noticed Dr. Dragonbreath's sad expression and said, "No, let's stay here and keep talking to Dr. Dragonbreath."

"I'm thirsty," said the second head.

"How do you keep forgetting your water bottle?" asked the eighth head.

Luckily for the snowboarders, five of the nine heads wanted to keep talking with Dr. Dragonbreath, so Ms. Hydra let the boys go. (It's important for a multi-headed lizard to have an odd number of heads so there's always a majority in decision making.)

The snowboarders were followed by a mob of students out into the deadly school yard.

The blanket of fresh white snow made the playground seem almost survivable in the early morning sunlight. The flowing river of lava had cooled into shiny black obsidian. The three friends pulled a switch-stance maneuver as they rode across the river of obsidian to the blazing volcano that fed the flowing lava.

The hardened lava created a vertical ramp up the face of the volcano, and Johnny, Ramon, and Peter rode up in a straight line, sending themselves skyward one hundred feet into the air!

In midair, each friend performed his best trick. Johnny pulled off a frontside double cork 1080, while Ramon managed to barely land a 720 barrel roll with a chicken salad grab! The best was saved for last, however, as Peter the Wolf landed the rare Double

McTwist 1260. The crowd went crazy, clapping their hands above their heads. Even several teachers were cheering.

Peter the Wolf led his two friends to the finish line. He drooled with anticipation of the kudos for their performance. In his exuberant mood, he transformed back to regular Peter. The crowd cheered even louder because they liked regular Peter much more than Peter the Wolf. Unfortunately, he didn't see that he was heading straight toward the Pit of Scarflakk, which was hidden by the fresh layer of snow.

Peter's height of joy fell to the depths of despair as he plunged into the Pit of Scarflakk—a ten-foot-wide hole in the ground with countless rings of razor-sharp teeth that ensnared its victims into its dark gullet, whence there was no escape.

If Peter the Wolf had fallen into the Pit of Scarflakk, nobody would have cared because Peter the Wolf was the meanest kid in school, but since regular Peter had fallen into the pit, everyone was devastated and prayed something could be done to save the nicest kid in school.

Dr. Dragonbreath tried to calm everyone down, saying, "Fear not, young humans. Peter is not dead yet. In the Scarflakk's belly he is merely going to experience a new definition of pain and suffering as he is slowly digested over a thousand years . . . wait . . . years? I meant seconds."

That made the students even more upset. Dr. Dragonbreath rolled his eyes, thinking, I don't know that I'll ever understand human emotions.

Princess Zogette stepped forward and announced in her stentorian, royalish voice, "I had a Pit of Scarflakk in my backyard at Monster Castle. There is but one way to rescue someone who has fallen into a Pit of Scarflakk, but it will require everyone's help to succeed. Also, you should know that Charles gave me a bouquet of flowers over Thanksgiving and they were beauuuutiful."

Charles retorted, "I didn't want to! My mom made me!"

Zogette went on to explain that Peter was no doubt already hundreds, if not thousands, of feet deep inside the long digestive tract of the Scarflakk. One person—a searcher—would have to go in first to locate him. It had to be someone who could see exceptionally well in the dark.

Penny Possum quickly volunteered. Her saucer-sized eyes were like night-vision goggles. Charles tried to object, but Penny spoke for the first time in months, saying "NO! I'M DOING THIS," knocking over half the students with the force of her voice.

"Okay then," said Zogette, "but she cannot go alone, or she would simply be digested herself. Someone must go with her—a protector—who can fend off the creepies that will try to snatch her."

Jason volunteered for that job. With his fearsome hockey mask and ever-present chainsaw, nothing stood a chance.

Zogette explained that once they found Peter deep down in the gullet, Penny and Jason would not be able to escape without help. The students would have to form a human chain in order to pull them to safety.

Everyone came to a quick agreement that the risk was worth it to save the life of their friend Peter. I tried not to take offense that no one had cared as much about saving my life a couple years ago, but whatever.

Penny Possum took the lead and made her way into the Pit of Scarflakk. Jason and his chainsaw followed close behind. After them, every student at Scary School began forming a human chain, holding on to one another by the ankles. It soon extended a thousand feet, keeping Penny and Jason connected to the surface.

The pit was pitch-dark, and every kid on the thousand-foot chain nearly barfed at the smell of thousand-year-old rotting meat, but Penny and Jason did their best to ignore the odor.

Monstrous little glow-in-the-dark creatures that looked like tiny devils kept popping up. They tried to grab hold of Penny and detach her from the chain, but Jason was swift with his chainsaw and made quick work of them.

After a long trek down the tube, where the smell grew even worse, Penny eventually found Peter. He had transformed into Peter the Wolf and was struggling for his life against an array of tentacles trying to pull him into a vat of bubbling acid—the Scarflakk's stomach!

Penny reached out her hand and took hold of Peter the Wolf's arm. Peter the Wolf could not see in the dark like Penny could and thought she was another tentacle. Peter thrashed at Penny's arm. Penny lost her grip and the tentacle pulled Peter closer to acid. He was barely out of Penny's reach.

Charles Nukid was holding onto Jason's ankles and yelled, "Jason! Take my tie!"

Jason nodded and sliced off Charlie's tie and handed it to Penny. Penny flung Charles's tie and it wrapped around Peter's wrist. She whispered to Jason that she had him.

News traveled like a game of telephone up the chain to the surface. There the strongest teachers, anchored by the mighty jaws of Ms. T (who was clasped on to

the tail of Dr. Dragonbreath), began pulling the chain of students out of the pit like a magician pulling a never-ending handkerchief out of his pocket.

After the chain of kids had wrapped around the entire school yard, Jason, Penny, and Peter the Wolf finally popped out of the hole to safety.

When the students noticed that they had gone through all that just to rescue Peter the Wolf, they groaned with disappointment. But when he changed back to regular Peter, they cheered with glee.

When Peter realized it was Charles's tie that had saved him, he handed it back and said, "That's the first time I was glad to wear a tie. Thanks, New Kid."

The reveling came to a quick end, however, when the sky rumbled and a great roar was heard. The students looked up and saw a fearsome winged creature flying toward them, ridden by what looked to be something pink and fuzzy.

The students in King Khufu's class quickly formed a circle around Bryce McCallister, hiding him from view. They were certain that death was about to arrive upon swift wings for him.

As it came closer, they realized it was Ms. Stingbottom riding atop a griffin—a lion with the head and wings of an eagle. The students let out a sigh of relief, thinking she was there to pay a friendly visit. When the griffin landed, they saw she looked frazzled and full of worry.

"Awoo-Aloo, my helpless humans!" Ms. Stingbottom bellowed, snapping her lobster claws and wiping tears off her furry pink face. "I bear terrible news. I have just flown past the one thousand pirate ships filled with monsters, and they are but a week away. That, I'm afraid, is the good news. The bad is that I have overheard their plans, and they are so furious at spending these last months at sea that when they arrive to do battle, they plan not only to retrieve Princess Zogette, but to *eat* anyone who dares resist them. That means there will be no coming back as a zombie, or a vampire, or a ghost, or a skeleton, for once you are eaten by a monster, that is simply the end of you. While before I encouraged you to fight for the love of Charles and Zogette—"

"Seriously. I don't like her," came a voice from the distance.

"—now, I have changed my mind and encourage all of you to surrender to the monsters. There is no hope of survival. Farewell."

In a blink, Ms. Stingbottom was flying back through the clouds on the griffin.

The students stood in stunned silence. They turned and looked at Charles Nukid and Princess Zogette.

"Welp, I guess that settles it," said Bryce McCallister. "You're a good dude, Charles, but you're going to have to give up your lady."

The princess cried out, "Noooo! You mustn't take me away from my Charles. I would rather die!"

The kids threw their arms up in exasperation.

That's when Petunia had the idea of a lifetime.

"Wait a minute," Petunia proclaimed, speaking louder than she ever had before. "We can't give up. The monsters have no right to invade our school. Zogette's father has no right to force her to marry someone she hates. Look at everything we have around us. The monsters won't know what to expect when they get here, but we know everything there is to know about the environment and all the traps that can be sprung. Divided, we stand no chance; but united, we form a chain that cannot be broken. Together we can teach those monsters an important life lesson about never messing with Scary School again!"

Johnny was so riled up by the speech, his feet grew two sizes. He felt like a real bigfoot for the first time. He released a roar, and all the students roared along with him.

If Petunia, an eleven-year-old purple girl, wasn't afraid of the monsters, then every kid figured there was no reason for them to be. Steven Kingsley felt no fear, Penny Possum felt no fear, Fritz felt no fear, and, of course, Fred, the boy without fear, still felt no fear.

Zogette gave Charles a big hug, and Charles nearly retched from her stench, but the moment was so overwhelming, something inside him began to feel differently. He reached out his arms and hugged Zogette back.

But only for a few seconds.

18

The All~Knowing Monkey of Scary Mountain

Before I tell you about the monster attack, it's important that you know the origin of one of Scary School's teachers. For as you will see, it is his story that will make all the difference.

On the final day of school last year, while Ms. Fangs's class was trapped inside the Room of Fun in Jacqueline's haunted house, the rest of the students met in the school yard for the presentation of their trophy for winning the Ghoul Games—the Golden Elephant.

Flying gargoyles lifted away the veil covering the

statue, revealing the magnificent figure. Shimmering in the sunlight, it stood on a thirty-foot pedestal, its trunk pointing to the sky, its ears large and floppy, its tusks as long as a mammoth's.

The elephant was the symbol of victory in the Scary community, for no human or monster had ever defeated one in battle. It was said that the golden elephant would ward off evil spirits and protect Scary School from bad luck.

Unfortunately, the next day, the elephant was gone.

What nobody knew was that the school yard of Scary School was built on top of an ancient Native American burial ground, which was itself built over an ancient mammoth graveyard, which was itself built over a *really* ancient dinosaur cemetery.

This explains the possessed merry-go-round, among many other freaky things at Scary School. Nothing built on the school grounds stands any chance of *not* becoming possessed, cursed, or haunted.

The day after the statue was unveiled, when school was out for the summer and everything was silent and empty, the spirits underneath the ground were tussling over who would get to possess the Golden Elephant statue. Eventually, a mammoth spirit from the mammoth graveyard won out, as was only fitting, since mammoths are the wooly ancestors of elephants.

The Golden Elephant came to life that same day. It hopped off the pedestal and landed with an earthshaking *thunk*. It wandered around the yard eating all the foliage on the trees as if it were a real elephant. Growing thirsty, it searched until it found Scary Pool.

Not realizing that gold sinks in water, it stepped in and immediately sank to the pool's murky depths, where the merpeople dwelled.

At first the merpeople were excited to receive a shiny new ornament for their underwater garden, but when they realized it was alive, they decided to save its life. Unfortunately, it was too heavy to lift back to the surface, even with all of them helping.

At the same time those merpeople were trying

193

to find a way to save the elephant, other mermaids and mermen were busy trying to revive Mr. Fishman. Mr. Fishman was one of Scary School's sixth-grade teachers. He was also a lagoon creature—dark green in color and looking like an odd mixture of a fish and a man. He had scaly skin, webbed limbs, and dorsal fins along his back and head.

Principal Headcrusher had ordered Mr. Fishman to put chlorine in Scary Pool so that it would be safe to swim in over the summer. Unfortunately, the piranhas took offense at this and dragged him into the water.

Covered with piranha bites, Mr. Fishman was moments from learning a valuable life lesson about not putting chlorine in piranha-infested waters as he was being bitten to pieces.

The merpeople saw that the only chance to save both the elephant's and Mr. Fishman's lives was to turn them into *one* life. They detached the Golden Elephant's head from its body. Underneath the gold plating was a regular elephant's body. The gold plating slipped off, and mersurgeons quickly attached the elephant head to Mr. Fishman's body.

Mr. Fishman's feet had also been bitten off by the piranhas, so they gave him some nice new elephant feet.

That's how he became Mr. Grump.

Mr. Grump (though he was not called that yet)

flapped his giant elephant ears, which quickly brought him up to the surface.

Sitting on the shore, he looked at his strange scaly hands and his stumpy elephant feet and realized he had no memory of who he was or where he came from. It was as if he had suddenly sprung into existence there on the bank of Scary Pool.

The only creature still inhabiting the Scary School grounds over summer vacation went over to investigate what was disturbing her solitude.

Tanya Tarantula approached Mr. Grump and stared at him quizzically. This was, of course, the summer before she fell into King Khufu's class on the fifth day of school.

Mr. Grump looked at Tanya with confusion. "Are you . . . my mother?" Mr. Grump asked.

Tanya shook her fangs back and forth.

"Do you know who I am or what I am?" Mr. Grump inquired.

It was then that Tanya spoke to another creature for the first time in her life. "I have heard it said that at the top of Scary Mountain lives a wise monkey that knows all."

Tanya pointed to the top of a snowy peak in the distance.

"Okay, I guess I better go there. Thanks." And

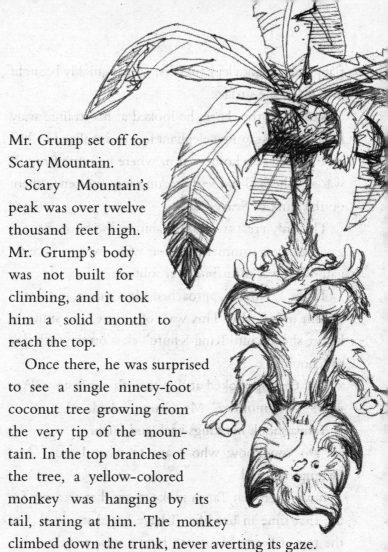

Mr. Grump set off for Scary Mountain.

Scary Mountain's peak was over twelve thousand feet high. Mr. Grump's body was not built for climbing, and it took him a solid month to reach the top.

Once there, he was surprised to see a single ninety-foot coconut tree growing from the very tip of the mountain. In the top branches of the tree, a yellow-colored monkey was hanging by its tail, staring at him. The monkey climbed down the trunk, never averting its gaze.

"Who do you think you are?" asked the monkey in a sharp tone.

"That's what I came here to ask *you*," replied Mr. Grump.

"Ohhh. So you seek answers from the All-Knowing Monkey of Scary Mountain?"

"Yes. Can you please tell me what I am?"

"Oh, I can. But I *won't*. You have to pay for that kind of valuable information. My beautiful coconut tree has run out of coconuts. Bring me some more, and I will tell you!"

"You can't get them on your own?"

"Oh, I *can* get them on my own, but I *won't* because I am very busy taking care of this tree. Coconut trees aren't supposed to grow this high up or in such cold weather. I have to constantly tell the tree it's growing in Hawaii. It's hard work!"

"Okay, fine. I'll get you some coconuts."

"And I want them in a big sack. No skimping. Now get out of here, you goofy eleph— Oops. I almost told you what you are."

197

Mr. Grump climbed back down the mountain, which only took him two weeks because going down was much easier. He found a coconut grove in Scary Forest, gathered as many coconuts as he could by ramming the trees with his thick skull, then spent another month climbing back up the snowy mountain, lugging the big sack of coconuts behind him.

When he reached the peak, the monkey was very excited to see him. It had grown thin, almost skeletal. It seemed Mr. Grump had arrived just in time.

"Thank you for coming back! I had almost given up hope," the monkey exclaimed with delight, devouring three coconuts right on the spot.

"Ahhh, that's much better," said the monkey, patting his belly. "I'm going to be smart and plant the rest of the coconuts. I'll have a flourishing grove in no time!"

"Good for you, Mr. Monkey. Now could you please tell me what I am?"

"Certainly. You are a lagoon creature with the head and feet of an elephant. Any other questions?"

"Uh . . . who am I?"

"You want a name, too? Okay, your name is . . . Morris Grump."

"I like it."

"Thank you. It was my mother's name. But you know, I think I got the better end of this bargain. So, let's say I still owe you one. Now get out of here, you elephant–lagoon monster." The monkey threw a coconut at Mr. Grump, causing him to tumble down Scary Mountain for another two weeks before reaching the bottom.

He wandered back to Scary School, the only other place he knew, but he had hit his head so many times on the way down, all he could remember was his new name and carrying that sack of coconuts up the mountain.

Little did Mr. Grump know that every kid in school would one day owe their lives to him for bringing the monkey that sack of coconuts.

It was the first day of school, and Principal Head-crusher was in a state of panic. Her sixth-grade teacher Mr. Fishman had not shown up. She needed to find a replacement. That's when she saw Mr. Grump wandering around the school yard. He looked like he was about to get sliced in half by the swinging ax on the jungle gym. Principal Headcrusher ran to him as fast as she could and yanked him out of the way.

"Mr. Fishman? Is that you?" she asked, seeing his lagoon-creature body.

"My name is Morris Grump," said Mr. Grump.

"Well, Mr. Grump, I suppose you look scary enough.

How would you like to teach sixth grade at this school?"

"Uhhh . . . okay."

"Fantastic! I'll get you a suit and everything you'll need. You're a real lifesaver."

"No problem. Wait . . . what's a sixth grade?"

Minutes later, Mr. Grump walked into his classroom. There he saw a little purple girl wearing a purple dress, sitting all alone.

The two weeks of tumbling down the mountain had caused him some significant memory problems, so by the time he reached the classroom, he had forgotten that he had just been hired to teach the sixth grade.

"Hello," said Mr. Grump to Petunia in his deep, goofy-sounding voice. "Are you the teacher?"

19

Friday the Thirteenth

It was a cold, sunny morning on Friday, December 13, at 8:00 a.m.—the day of the attack.

Nobody liked the idea that the monsters would be attacking on Friday the thirteenth, but there certainly wasn't anything that could be done about it. Jason was the only one who thought it was a good omen.

The Scary School students had been working all week to form a plan of defense. Staying home to avoid the attack was not an option. That would be like leaving a friend to die on the field of battle.

FRIDAY
DECEMBER
13

NOTE: Get Invaded

By the end of the week, every student knew where they needed to be and what they needed to do. The plan had to work to perfection if they were to survive.

All the students had arrived half an hour early to rehearse the plan one last time and take their positions.

Meanwhile, ten thousand monsters marched in formation toward the front entrance of Scary School. There were five thousand karate monsters, well-trained in the deadliest forms of martial arts, and five thousand monster-pirates, not well-trained in anything, but bloodthirsty nonetheless.

Just as Ms. Stingbottom had warned, all ten thousand were wearing earplugs.

Closer and closer they marched, drums pounding and flags waving.

The smell of ten thousand garbage trucks dumping their loads in the middle of a skunk convention grew stronger by the second. The overwhelming stench signaled the time was at hand.

The front lawn of Scary School was soon to be a historic battleground.

When the monsters arrived, it was quiet and virtually empty, save for one student.

Charles Nukid.

Charles stood proud and unflinching. He wore his gray shorts, white dress shirt, and polka-dot tie—the school uniform that everyone else refused to wear. If he was going to die, he was going to die following the rules. He stared with defiance at the massive army before him.

Charles calmly patted his head to make sure no

hairs were out of place.

Ten thousand monsters bared their lethal fangs and raised their sharp swords.

Charles Nukid, who looked more like a oversized toothpick than a human boy, raised his two fists and said:

"Bring it on."

20

The Monsters Attack

The ten thousand monsters were flabbergasted by the boldness of the skinny kid in front of them. Their claws and teeth were twitching and tingling in anticipation of shredding him like paper and eating him alive!

King Zog and Captain Pigbeard emerged from the ranks. The king's animal-hide robe was sparkling with jewels. His skull crown was resting proudly atop his fat toad head. The scent of fresh lilacs was wafting off his body.

Captain Pigbeard stood next to him dressed in full

pirate regalia. The rings on his tusks and snout were shimmering in the sunlight.

"Yar! Ye be the boy who has stolen my hideous bride!" Pigbeard declared.

"You have also taken King Zog's daughter without permission!" King Zog hollered from atop the hill, pompously referring to himself in the third person.

"Yeah. What are you going to do about it?" Charles Nukid replied.

The monsters growled in disbelief.

King Zog shouted, "None of your friends have come to support you. But King Zog is not without a heart. Give Zogette back to us, and King Zog shall let you live."

"No! You are trespassing on Scary School property. Be gone from here, and *I* shall let *you* live."

The monsters broke out in laughter.

"Avast!" shouted Captain Pigbeard. "This be your last chance. Tell me where be my bride!"

"Never!"

King Zog raised his scepter. "Very well, then. Monsters . . . ATTAAAAAACK!"

Elated at the order, ten thousand monsters roared as loud as they could.

Captain Pigbeard raised his sword in front of the five thousand monster-pirates. The monster-pirates raised their own swords in response. They were dressed in frilly pirate costumes with puffy shirts, pantaloons, tricorn hats, eye patches, and jackets with gold buttons. Their horns jutted through holes in their hats, and their claws poked through their boots. The eight nearest Charles rampaged toward him crying out "Yaaar!" and "Aye, matey!"

Charles turned and ran as fast as he could toward the front entrance of the school. The monster-pirates were quickly closing the gap behind him. Charles crossed the drawbridge, but when the pirates got there, eight fearsome tentacles shot out of the moat, snatching the monster-pirates with immense suckers.

The captured monster-pirates squealed and writhed, but could not escape. Archie pulled them into the water and had a very satisfying breakfast. Giant squids like eating pirates because they taste like seafood.

Captain Pigbeard squealed with rage. He ordered the rest of the monster-pirates into Scary School's front entrance. Charles stood at the end of the hallway making faces to tease them into attacking recklessly. The monster-pirates charged, but the floors had been coated with a fine layer of water from Marvin the ogre's new mop bucket. They slipped backward, falling on their pirate pantaloons. As they crashed on top of one another, a mass of third graders leaped out of

the lockers. Working together, they lifted the monster-pirates and threw them into the lockers, shutting the doors and trapping them helplessly inside.

Captain Pigbeard was furious. This time, he himself led the monster-pirates inside to capture Charles. Pigbeard entered the hallway much more cautiously.

Again, Charles appeared and made a face at them. The fastest monster-pirate ran after Charles. But just before the monster could grab hold of Charles's collar, the vile green claw lunged out of Locker 39. It grabbed the stunned monster-pirate by its horns, and pulled it into the Locker of Infinite Oblivion.

Charles was almost at the next checkpoint. The rest of the monster-pirates continued to press down the hallway roaring, "Yarrr!" Suddenly, dozens of fourth graders emerged from their classrooms. They aimed what looked like water pistols at the monster-pirates.

The monster-pirates halted and started laughing. "Har! Har! Har!"

Captain Pigbeard exclaimed, "Do ye really expect to stop us with a little spray of water? You scalawags shall be tasty appetizers!"

But as the monster-pirates advanced, the fourth graders lowered gas masks over their faces and shot the liquid from their pistols onto the floor. Exposed to the air, the liquid immediately turned into a thick gas, which the monster-pirates could not help but breathe in. The fourth graders had doused them with Fear Gas—the very same gas that exploded in Mr. Acidbath's class two years ago, ending the life of yours truly.

As soon as it entered their lungs, the monster-pirates froze in their tracks. Their eyes darted back and forth.

"Everything is so scary here!" Pigbeard shrieked. The monster-pirates huddled together, shaking.

I decided to become visible at that moment and shouted, "Boo!"

Screaming in terror, Pigbeard and his horde retreated back to their pirate ships many miles away, where they jumped into their beds and pulled the covers over themselves.

Charles and the fourth graders danced with joy. They gave so many high fives, their hands were hurting! They tried to high-five me as well, but they went right through me and smacked their friends in the face.

Seeing the monster-pirates defeated, King Zog was as startled as he was furious.

Unfortunately for the children of Scary School, there were still five thousand of Zog's elite soldiers—the karate monsters—who would not be so easily fooled.

The karate monsters looked vicious and disciplined. They wore different-colored karate belts indicating their level of expertise. Most were odd combinations of trolls and warthogs, orcs and hyenas, gremlins and gorillas.

Zog decided to lead the force himself to ensure capture of the elusive Charles Nukid.

The karate monsters circled around the sides of the school, heading for where Charles stood at the back entrance. As planned, he was met by Johnny, Ramon, and Peter with their skateboards.

The monsters crept around both corners of the building, grinning when they spotted the boys standing there helpless. Zog gave the order, and they charged full speed ahead. Charles jumped onto Johnny the Sasquatch's shoulders. Charles and the three friends took off on their skateboards as the monsters chased after them. Then they ollied onto metal rails they had installed that week and slid across the yard at breakneck speed.

"Yahoo!" said Charles, thinking this was the

most fun ride of his life.

The dumbstruck monsters tripped over themselves trying to catch up.

The rails ended at Scary Pool, where Fritz was waiting. Their parts done, Johnny, Ramon, and Peter wished Charles luck and skated off. The karate monsters finally caught up and charged toward Charles and Fritz.

Fritz lowered his goggles. Charles climbed onto his back, and Fritz swam with him to the middle of Scary Pool.

The monsters surrounded the banks of Scary Pool. "They have to come out sometime!" said King Zog, chuckling.

But then Charles and Fritz rose up out of the water on the head of Nessie, the Loch Ness Monster. Nessie swept her tail through the water, sending a fifty-foot tidal wave careening toward the battalion of monsters.

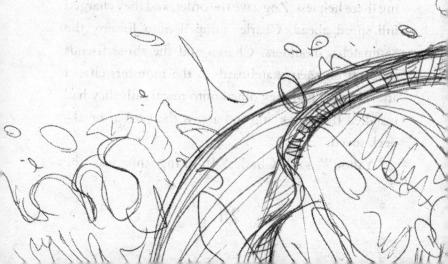

"Uh-oh," said the monsters, as the wave crashed down upon them. Thousands of monsters were washed away by the tide and then sucked back into the pool, where they were attacked by the hungry piranhas!

Charles and Fritz high-fived. Nessie extended her eighty-foot neck like a bridge over the gates of Scary Pool, allowing Fritz and Charles to hop off her nose in a safe area. Fritz tossed a bucket of fish into Nessie's mouth as a reward. "Thanks, Nessie!" said Fritz. Nessie licked him with her long tongue, and Fritz would smell like fish for the rest of his life.

Charles made his way back to the school yard. The monsters who had escaped Scary Pool were hot on his trail.

King Zog roared with fury. Each time it seemed Charles was in his grasp, he managed a miraculous escape.

Penny Possum was waiting for Charles at the Pit of Scarflakk. They held hands and jumped into the pit together. Charles hardly remembered what it felt like to hold Penny's hand and he relished the moment.

King Zog ordered his karate monsters to crawl into the pit after Charles and Penny, thinking it was just an ordinary hole in the ground.

Once the last monster was in the pit, the Scary School kids emerged from hiding and quickly formed a human chain. The chain of kids slinked inside the pitch-dark pit. The pit already smelled like rotting meat, and with the added odors of hundreds of monsters, it was all but unbearable.

The students ventured bravely and nauseously down the pit's long throat, led by Jason and his reliable chainsaw. Penny saw her friends coming for them while hiding at the edge of the Scarflakk's belly. She grabbed hold of Jason's free hand, and she and Charles were pulled out to safety.

The monsters had no one to pull them out. Thus they were trapped in the pit and slowly digested over a thousand years . . . I mean seconds.

The pit was beyond full and burped with satisfaction.

For a few moments, the students believed they had succeeded. They ran up to Charles and Penny and patted them on the back and gave them hugs.

But then, King Zog clapped his hands from high on his mobile throne. Thunder crashed and five hundred more monsters were lowered through the clouds in the claws of giant vultures.

These monsters looked bigger, meaner, and more athletic than any of the other monsters.

"You have fought bravely," said King Zog from his throne. "But as you can see, King Zog has saved his most elite karate monsters for last. These are the monsters who have never lost in battle, and King Zog assures you, they

215

will tear you all to pieces if given the order."

The students looked at one another, checking if anyone had a plan other than begging for mercy.

The tension was snapped when Mr. Grump trumpeted his trunk and galumphed out in front of the students.

The monsters flinched at the elephant man's strange appearance.

"Move out of the way, you . . . odd creature," barked King Zog. "Our fight is not with you. In fact, you would make a fine addition to Monster Kingdom."

"Nuh-uh. You won't harm a single hair on any of my students' heads."

"If you refuse to move, you shall be devoured along with them."

Mr. Grump got nervous realizing it was just him versus five hundred monsters, but then the doors burst open and Principal Headcrusher emerged. She stood next to Mr. Grump. "Then you'll have to go through me too," she decreed, forming her giant hands into fists.

All of a sudden, the rest of the teachers came out and joined the formation—Dr. Dragonbreath and Ms. Hydra, Mrs. T the T. rex, Ms. Fangs, King Khufu, and Mr. Snakeskin. Even Tanya Tarantula joined the line to defend all her new friends.

Dr. Dragonbreath spoke in his stern dragon voice: "Nobody eats students at Scary School but us."

21
The Curse Comes True

King Zog smiled his stumpy-toothed smile, stood up on his horse legs, and raised his scorpion tail. He didn't seem at all intimidated by the line of Scary School teachers.

"Ha! Ha! Ha! For teachers, you have made a very unwise choice. Monsters . . . attaaack!"

The elite karate monsters released their furious war cries and charged forward. Mr. Grump instinctually did an elephant charge, blasting through their front line. Mrs. T swung her tail, whacking thirty monsters at once, sending them flying into the air. Dr.

Dragonbreath and Ms. Hydra blew a wall of fire to keep the karate monsters away from the students.

The karate monsters were displaying their moves, aiming flying kicks and powerful chops at Scary School's protectors.

Twenty monsters pounced upon Mr. Grump to subdue him. Unable to shake the monsters off, the only thing that squeezed through the pile was Mr. Grump's pliable trunk. With the last breath he could muster, he trumpeted as loud as he could.

The sound of his trumpet traveled across the landscape at the speed of . . . well . . . sound, until it reached the ears of the All-Knowing Monkey of Scary Mountain. Lounging in his coconut tree, which had recently become an entire grove of coconut trees thanks to Mr. Grump, the startled All-Knowing Monkey surveyed the melee below with his binoculars. "Oh no! Morris Grump is in trouble. I got your back, buddy."

Tanya Tarantula was doing her best to fend off a horde of monsters with her giant fangs. She raised her legs, and sharp hairs shot out like darts, flying right into the eyes of the monsters, who dropped to their knees in anguish.

Wow, thought Tanya. I didn't even know I could do that. But then, a swarm of tarantula hawks emerged from the monster multitude. The highly poisonous wasps descended upon Tanya, who had no good defense against such small creatures. With her eight eyes, she noticed that these were the very same tarantula hawks that had killed 490 of her brothers and sisters. They had come to finish the job.

The tarantula hawks laughed in their buzzy language. "Hee hee hee! You thought you could escape from us, but we knew we'd find you one day!"

The tarantula hawks surged toward Tanya, their stingers full of venom aimed at her vulnerable abdomen. Tanya closed her eight eyes, thinking this was the end. But at the last second, another giant tarantula emerged from the fray. It was as big as a car!

The huge tarantula shot a net of silk from its backside. The net ensnared the tarantula hawks in a sticky, inescapable cocoon.

Tanya opened her eight eyes and saw the snared insects. The giant tarantula in front of her waved and Tanya recognized her immediately.

It was her mother.

Tears poured out from all sixteen of the mother and daughter's eyes, and they shared a big tarantula hug.

"Mommy, you do care!" Tanya exclaimed through tears of joy.

Tanya's mother didn't know how to talk, but she

nodded her fangs up and down as fast as she could.

Despite their early success, the Scary School teachers were becoming overwhelmed by the sheer number of monsters. Dr. Dragonbreath, Ms. Hydra, Principal Headcrusher, and Mrs. T had been taken captive. The rest were close to meeting a similar fate. Only Mr. Grump was still struggling beneath the pile of monsters on top of him, laboring with his last ounce of strength to burst free.

That was when the miracle happened. There was a great rumbling on the ground. By the time the monsters turned around, it was too late. Hundreds upon hundreds of coconuts were rolling straight at them faster than race cars. Without time to dive out of the way, the monsters were smacked by the coconuts like bowling pins.

The All-Knowing Monkey had rolled them all the way down Scary Mountain with pinpoint precision. The coconuts were extra hard and icy from growing on the snowcap, which had made them as solid as cannonballs.

The monkey shrieked with glee, performing monkey flips when he witnessed his perfect strike.

Only two monsters had managed to avoid the bombardment: King Zog, perched high on his throne, and a bearodactyl—the lone winged monster remaining.

It had flown upward to avoid the collision.

From high in the air, the bearodactyl recognized Charles Nukid. It was the same mama bearodactyl that had mistakenly thought Charles was after her offspring in Monster Forest. She saw it was the perfect opportunity to finish Charles off and teach him an important life lesson about not messing with bearodactyl babies.

The bearodactyl, with its sharp pterodactyl beak, razor teeth, and powerful wings, went into a nosedive, barreling toward the defenseless Charles. He was cheering so fervently after the coconut collision, he did not realize that all his classmates had seen the bearodactyl and had taken cover.

Bryce McCallister noticed that Charles was oblivious to his imminent doom. He decided this was the perfect opportunity to repay him for keeping the secret about his uncursed state. Bryce brushed his long hair out of his eyes, then leaped in front of Charles, selflessly taking the brunt of the bearodactyl's attack.

As Bryce was gored by the furious monster, the girls in King Khufu's class screamed. This was the moment they had been dreading all year. The curse of death coming to Bryce upon swift wings had come true, even though there was actually no curse at all.

Luckily, the Scary School medic, Nurse Hairymoles, was the best nurse in the whole world. She quickly pulled Bryce off to the side and turned him into a vampire before his body could start decaying. Bryce's long hair and dark good looks suited him becoming a vampire perfectly.

Now the girls in Bryce's class liked him even more than before.

Meanwhile, Charles was running for his life from the angry bearodactyl. But the bearodactyl easily knocked Charles to the ground. Charles found himself cornered between the Scary School building and a large Dumpster, with nowhere left to run. The bearodactyl smiled and drooled over the delicious meal it would soon be enjoying, when a loud voice was heard from high above.

"Nooo! Not my Charles!" the not-quite-royal voice cried out.

Princess Zogette leaped from the top of Scary School's roof, where she had been hiding the whole time, falling bottom-first upon the bearodactyl like a ton of bricks. The bearodactyl was knocked out by

Tongue
of Doom!

Zogette's bottom, teaching it a very important life lesson about not messing with Zogette's man.

Charles looked up at the princess and could only say, "You saved my life."

Zogette smiled at Charles and fixed three hairs on his head that had gone out of place.

But before Charles could even give her a thank-you hug, a sticky tongue hit Zogette right in the back and yanked her away.

22

The Big Kiss

K ing Zog had seen his chance and shot his impossibly long frog's tongue across the yard, reeling Zogette in like a fish.

"At last I have you back, insolent daughter!" King Zog proclaimed. "Now it is time to marry Captain Pigbeard!"

"No, Father! Please don't make me do it!" Zogette pleaded.

"Who you marry is not your choice. As your father, it is *my* choice. No more arguments."

King Zog jumped off his throne, holding Zogette

tightly to his chest. He began running toward the coast with his speedy horse legs.

Nobody was sure whether or not to get in the middle of this family issue. The monsters had been defeated, so the teachers and students seemed to think that the battle was over.

The only one who couldn't stand to see Zogette abducted was Petunia. She knew what it felt like to be held against her will from her time in Scary Forest last year. She ordered the bees and wasps buzzing around her hair to stop King Zog.

The bees flew after King Zog while Petunia and Charles ran to catch up. When the bees swarmed the king, they halted his escape. He was shrieking from the stings and swatting the bees away.

"Don't take another step!" Petunia shouted. "You have no right to force your daughter to marry someone she doesn't want to be with."

The bees drew away from King Zog, but remained hovering around him to make sure he didn't try to run off again.

"Little purple girl," said King Zog, "you do not understand monster customs. Zogette must marry whoever I choose, for her own good and for the good of the monster species."

"No, she must not," Petunia replied. "Marriage

is about more than political arrangements. It's about love."

"I do not know of this human emotion called *love*. It sounds very silly."

"When you were a young monster, your parents freed you from the dungeon because they loved you. When you waged battle against the Monster King Bub-Gub to save your parents from his dungeon, did you not do that out of love?"

"You're saying . . . how I feel for my parents . . . that's how Zogette and Charles feel for each other?"

"Well . . . it's a different kind of love, but it's still love. By separating Charles and Zogette, you are doing the same thing that the intolerant monsters did to you and your parents. You are no better than them."

King Zog was taken aback. He had never thought that what he was doing could possibly cause so much pain to his daughter. He thought she had just wanted to annoy him.

"Okay," said King Zog. "I want to see this *love* you speak of." King Zog released Zogette. "If Zogette and Charles proclaim their love for each other and share a tender kiss, *maybe* I will believe in it."

Charles began sweating bullets. This whole time he had put up with Zogette because he wanted to follow the rules and because he felt bad for her. He never

really liked her. Now he had to convince King Zog that what they had was true love.

"Fine! I agree, Father!" Zogette declared. "Come to me, Charles."

Charles walked slowly to Zogette. She stood there smiling with her misshapen teeth and her slimy frog tongue hanging out, giggling with anticipation.

As soon as Charles reached her, she took his hands and proclaimed, "I love you, Charles! Now, you say it."

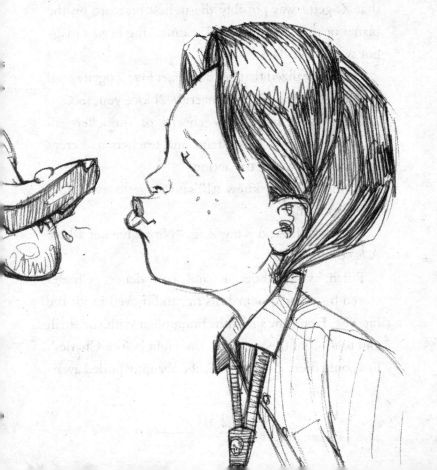

At that moment, a flood of images went through Charles's head. He remembered the big hug Zogette gave him when he saved her from the monster-pirates. He remembered the amazing guitar she gave to him, signed by all his favorite musicians. He remembered her eating the entire Thanksgiving turkey in one gulp. He remembered her making a brave leap from the top of Scary School's roof to save his life just minutes ago. And suddenly, Charles did not care anymore that Zogette was possibly the ugliest creature on the planet or that she smelled like something even a maggot would not dare to eat.

Charles realized that he did in fact love Zogette, and told her with the deepest sincerity, "I love you, too."

"Awwww," sounded a chorus of onlookers all around Charles. The students and teachers had crept up quietly to watch the action.

"Oh, Charles! I knew it!" said Zogette, swooning with emotion.

"Very well," said King Zog. "Now give her a kiss. A *big* one."

Filled with jubilation and confidence, Charles closed his eyes, loosened his tie, and moved in for the big kiss. Everyone's mouths hung open with the thrill and tension of the moment. But right before Charles's lips could meet Zogette's . . . she abruptly pulled away.

Charles opened his eyes in confusion. Zogette's joyous expression had changed to a look of puzzlement and uncertainty.

"Uh-oh," she said. "Aaaawkward."

"What's wrong?" Charles asked.

"Listen," Zogette said. "You're a really great guy. I've had a really good time with you. But, um . . . this just isn't working out."

"Huh? What do you mean?"

"Look, this relationship is over. But you're super nice, and I hope we can still be friends. I'm going to go back with my dad now and marry Captain Pigbeard. Deep down I guess I still have feelings for him. Send me an email sometime and let me know how you're doing, okay?"

Charles just stood there in shock as Zogette turned around and walked back toward her father.

Dr. Dragonbreath, Charles's favorite teacher, walked up behind Charles and patted him on the back.

"Funny thing about monsters," said Dr. Dragonbreath. "They only want what they can't have."

"So, as soon as I actually liked her, she lost interest in me?"

"Welcome to life, kid."

"Ugh," Petunia piped in. "I can't believe she's going to marry that monster-pirate after all this."

"Oh, I wouldn't count on it," said Dr. Dragon-breath. "Now that she wants to be with him, he won't want to be with her anymore. The most successful monster marriages are the ones where neither of the two monsters wants to be together at all."

Of course, as soon as Zogette went willingly back to her father, her father suddenly had an urge to be rid of her as well.

"Hey!" said King Zog. "Are you sure you don't want to keep Zogette here at Scary School? The castle was so nice and quiet without her there."

"Oh hush, Father!" Princess Zogette huffed, bopping him on his toad head. "Take me back to the ship. If Pigbeard won't have me, I'm moving back in with you."

"Ohhhhhh . . . ," King Zog grumbled. "What was I thinking?"

23
A Happy Holiday

Since the historic Friday the Thirteenth Battle
had ended by late morning, the students had the
rest of the day to party before going on holiday
break.

During the holiday party, Charles Nukid gave Penny
Possum a candy cane. He was very happy to see that
Penny had brought one for him too. The exchange
reminded them of how they first became friends.

Knowing that they could face down ten thousand
monsters and come out victorious gave the students of
Scary School an amazing feeling of pride. They had

proven that if you put enough effort into it, you can do absolutely anything.

Principal Headcrusher stole away from the party and collapsed in her office chair. She breathed a deep sigh of relief, her eyes welling up with tears, realizing that her school had survived its greatest threat to date. One of her tears landed on an envelope that she hadn't noticed was there.

It was postmarked from the Arctic Circle. She opened the envelope with her teeth and read the letter.

Dear Principal Headcrusher,

If any of your students have survived the monster attack, we would like to cordially invite them to be a part of our study abroad program and attend school at your alma mater, Scream Academy, which is still widely considered the scariest school in the world. We assume your answer is a resounding YES and we will be sending a representative to Scary School after winter break to judge which students are worthy of the program.

Best of luck surviving the monster attack.

Sincerely,
Rolf Meltington the Abominable Snowman
Principal
Scream Academy, aka the Aaaaaa!cademy

Principal Headcrusher plopped her head into her enormous hands. She would have to do her best to make this winter break her dream vacation, for once school resumed, it looked to be the beginning of a brand-new nightmare.

On Christmas Eve, Charles Nukid's phone rang. He answered it, but heard nothing on the other end. He knew exactly who it was.

After several moments of silence, Charles replied:

"Happy holidays to you too, Penny."

Final Note from
Derek the Ghost

ongratulations!
	Looks like you've survived the first part of the new school year.

I had high hopes for you, and you didn't let me down.

As a reward, I have a very special surprise for you. I was floating around the empty halls of Scary School over winter break and took a quick glance inside Locker 39—the Locker of Infinite Oblivion. Inside it, I saw that Steven Kingsley had hidden his new story, called "The Rainbow and the Kittens." Don't let the title fool you. I hear it's even sillier than it sounds.

If you want to read it, go to ScarySchool.com and look for Locker 39. If you click on it, you'll get to open the locker and read the story before anyone else!

Plus, if you look around carefully, you'll be able to find some of the other books I've written that you can only get on the website.

See you there!

Derek the Ghost

Join Charles Nukid and his friends
for another year at the scariest school
on earth in

for another year at the scariest school
on earth in

1

Vacation Is Over

Petunia walked into Dungeon 5B five minutes before class started on the first day of school after winter break. She breathed a sigh of relief that the rest of her sixth-grade classmates were already in their seats. On the first day of school after summer break, her classroom had been empty, which led to a very scary rescue in Jacqueline's haunted house. She had no desire to go back there.

Frank (which is pronounced "Rachel") was fixing her brown, frizzy hair when Petunia entered. Frank jumped up out of her seat to hug her but recoiled when she saw that Petunia's long purple hair was once again swarming with bees. So they high-fived from a safe distance.

"Hi, Petunia! I missed you so much! Did you get any good presents for the holidays?"

"Just some new books," Petunia replied.

"I got a new jump rope that has an automatic counter. I got up to sixteen million jumps by New Year's Eve. Using Monster Math that's like—"

"Fifty-five trillion jumps," a voice answered.

Petunia and Frank turned around to see a girl wearing all black.

"Oh, hey," said Petunia. "You must be new. I'm Petunia. What's your name?"

"My name is swiftness. My name is stealth. I will know these like I know my name," the girl in black replied in a deadly serious tone.

Petunia and Frank looked at each other and shrugged.

"Ooookay," said Frank. "How do you know Monster Math?"

"My master was the greatest monster mathematician who ever lived. An evil dragon the size of a mountain took him from me. Have you seen this dragon?"

Petunia and Frank looked at each other again.

"Umm . . . no," they replied.

The girl in black squinted her eyes. Then she asked, "Is this the class of the one called King Khufu?"

Petunia replied, "No, that's the other sixth-grade class."

In a blink, the girl in black vanished. Don't worry; there will be much more about her very soon.

As Petunia took her seat, she looked around the room. As usual, Penny Possum was sitting in the back corner, trying to go unnoticed. Fritz was wearing his swim goggles and swim trunks, hoping he would get to take a dip in Scary Pool.

Petunia waved to Jason, who wore his hockey mask and kept his chainsaw stowed inside his desk. She waved to Johnny, who was nibbling at an itch on his furry Sasquatch foot.

Neither boy waved back to Petunia.

They didn't intend to be mean. They were just scared that it might incite the bees swarming around Petunia's head to attack. They nodded back ever so slightly, noticing Petunia's long purple hair draping down her purple shoulders and over her purple dress.

Petunia liked purple. A lot. But since she was completely purple from head to foot, she didn't really have much choice.

Fred, the boy without fear, strolled down the

aisle, cool and relaxed, wearing his baggy jeans and backward cap.

Petunia noticed Lindsey, Stephanie, and Maria looking at Fred dreamily and felt a twinge of . . . something. She couldn't quite label it. Fred stopped by Johnny's desk and helped him scratch the itch with his long sharpened fingernails.

"Aaaah," said Johnny, relieved. "Thanks!"

Fred laughed. "There's definitely no such thing as a talking Sasquatch. Looks like I'm still dreaming."

Yep, everything seemed back to normal, as if King Zog's attack on the school just a few weeks ago was a distant memory.

Suddenly, a stomping from outside shook the room. It was the warning that their teacher, Mr. Grump, was approaching. Petunia hoped his memory had improved enough over the break that he would at least

remember he was the teacher.

As Mr. Grump stomped into the room, everyone rushed to their seats. He was a very nice teacher, but the class knew that if a lagoon creature with the head of an elephant got angry, he'd have no problem charging at them, tusks first.

Mr. Grump seemed puzzled as he looked at the students. No surprise there. Puzzled was the most common expression on his face. He looked at a piece of paper in his hand. Then he looked back at the students. It was obvious he had no idea who or where he was. Then he stomped down the aisle and took a seat at one of the open desks. The chair was way too small for him and it shattered into a thousand pieces as soon as he sat on it.

"Ouch!" said Mr. Grump. "I have splinters in my bottom."

Petunia rolled her eyes and went over to help him up. She was the only student who he could consistently remember.

"Hello, Petunia," said Mr. Grump with a smile.

"Hi, Mr. Grump. You shouldn't be sitting there. You're the teacher. Remember?"

"No, I don't think so," Mr. Grump replied. "Look."

Mr. Grump handed Petunia the piece of paper.

"What does it say?" asked Wendy Crumkin, the smartest girl in class. She brushed back her red hair and pushed up her glasses over her freckled nose.

Petunia responded, "It's a note from Principal Headcrusher. It says, 'Dear Mr. Grump. It has come to my attention that you know absolutely nothing and are therefore not qualified to be a teacher at this school. However, you are welcome to join your class as a student. As soon as you know *something* instead of *nothing*, I will consider rehiring you. Yours truly, Principal Meredith Headcrusher.'"

Ramon, the zombie kid, blurted, "But . . . if he's not the teacher, then who—" Ramon's zombie jaw fell off his face in the middle of his sentence. He quickly scooped it off the ground and reattached it. "Sorry. As I was saying . . . then who is the teacher?"

The clock struck eight a.m., and a cackling was heard from outside the door. "Heh-heh-heh-heh-heh!"

The students looked at one another and gulped. The identity of their teacher was going to be a surprise, and nobody liked surprises at Scary School. If you were the recipient of a surprise, the bigger surprise would be if you still had all your arms and legs a moment later.

Suddenly, the door was kicked open, and an old man wearing a long white lab coat stumbled into the classroom. In his arms he carried dozens of beakers and jars full of colorful bubbling chemicals.

The beakers and jars were piled so high they nearly touched the ceiling. They wobbled back and forth and looked like they were about to come crashing down at any moment.

The items were blocking the teacher's face, so nobody could tell who it was. But then the teacher set the beakers down on his desk and emerged from behind them.

"Hello, class!" exclaimed the teacher in a high-pitched, maniacal voice. "I'm baaaack!"

The entire class screamed at the same time. Penny Possum fell to the ground and played dead.

It was Mr. Acidbath.